Wilfrid Meynell

## John Henry Newman

The Founder of Modern Anglicanism and a Cardinal of the Roman Church

Wilfrid Meynell

**John Henry Newman**
*The Founder of Modern Anglicanism and a Cardinal of the Roman Church*

ISBN/EAN: 9783744674379

Printed in Europe, USA, Canada, Australia, Japan

Cover: Foto ©Raphael Reischuk / pixelio.de

More available books at **www.hansebooks.com**

# John Henry Newman

## THE FOUNDER OF

## MODERN ANGLICANISM

### AND

## A CARDINAL OF THE ROMAN CHURCH

BY

## WILFRID MEYNELL

*WITH PORTRAIT*

LONDON

KEGAN PAUL, TRENCH, TRÜBNER & CO., LtD

1890

# DEDICATION.

——◦◦——

## To the Very Rev. WILLIAM LOCKHART,
### Of the Institute of Charity.

My dear Father Lockhart,

Your secession from the Church of England, while you were under Dr. Newman's care at Littlemore, was the immediate cause of his resignation of the Vicarage of St. Mary's. You, then, had the glory of leading, and he the glory of following where you led. When one remembers what small causes bring large results, it is worth while to record that you yourself owed your conversion to a chance encounter with a book in the keeping of an undergraduate of St. John's College —now known as Father Ignatius Grant, S.J. That book was Milner's "End of Controversy," and it was the beginning of the end of controversy for you.

So, in linking your name with that of Cardinal Newman, I am only recalling a passage in the personal history of the great Oxford Movement towards the Church of the Apostles. I hope you will think I can with equal fitness associate your dear and honoured name with any publication of mine; since it was under the cover of your friendship, fifteen years ago, that my first scribbler's tasks were taken in hand. Allow me, then, to offer this public expression of gratitude and of love to one who has done favours to so many and is by many so greatly loved.

I am, my dear Father Lockhart,

Always affectionately yours,

WILFRID MEYNELL.

# AUTHOR'S PREFACE.

My first intention, in beginning this record, was merely to get together some reminiscences of the places most closely associated with Cardinal Newman—some of them already places of pilgrimage. But before I came to the end of it, the history of his habitations had grown into a Monograph. In speaking of the place I had told of the man who made it memorable while the association lasted. Anecdotes and reminiscences wove themselves into the text, and I found that I had made a sort of *mémoire pour servir.*

For the moment, therefore, these pages may be welcome to some as containing the completest record yet made of the movements and surroundings of Cardinal Newman all his life long. I hasten to add my grateful acknowledgments to those to whom alone that completeness is due: friends and companions of the Cardinal who have given me their aid: the Rev. Frederic S. Bowles first among them all. It remains to be said that, in treating the same incidents over again, I have not been at pains to vary the wording from that , already used in articles contributed to the *Athenæum*, to the *Contemporary Review*, and (under a pen-name) to *Merry England*.

PALACE COURT, LONDON, W.,
*September*, 1890.

# CONTENTS.

# CARDINAL NEWMAN.

## CHAPTER I.

### EARLY HOMES AND HAUNTS.

The Cardinal's father—An unsuccessful career—The promise
of its fruits—"A Mother of Men"—Studious sisters—
The one dead of a long-lived family—Frank Newman
and a growing asunder—Charles Newman and a swift
division—Uneventful youth—Brief and various homes
—Travelling with preoccupations—Hither and thither
in the years to come.

BANKING, in modern England at any rate, is
associated with philanthropy and generally with
Evangelicalism. Strange to say, three of the most
illustrious converts to the Catholic Church in the
early middle of this century were sons of men connected with those innermost shrines of Babylon,
London banks—Manning, Newman, Ward. Like
bankers, brewers also, by some freak of restitu-
tional justice, are men mostly given to good works
—out of the brewery. Cardinal Newman's father

first banked, then brewed, and failed at both. It was not that he allowed his Freemasonry, or his music, or his scheme for the reafforesting of England, to distract him from business; for after the bank in Lombard Street broke during a financial crisis, he became the slave of his brewery at Alton —to no purpose. There is something melancholy, in the picture of the man who deserves, but does not command, success; nor does Cato's encouragement avail him. What real comfort Mr. John Newman had, he had from his son, John Henry, who was able to give him the good news of his election to a Fellowship at Oriel in 1823. The father died soon afterwards, a man disappointed in himself, and not realizing the greatness which awaited the son who bore his name. /He was a Cambridge man by birth. The family had been small proprietors of land; but it was Newman's want of "high connections" that placed the aristocratic Pusey at the nominal head of the Oxford Movement.

Jemima Fourdrinier, when she married John Newman in 1799, brought her husband a small fortune, which, after the bank and brewery went, was all that remained for the family to live upon, until John Henry's earnings swelled the slender purse. Of Huguenot descent, and belonging to a family of famous paper-makers, whose plate still appears on Ludgate Hill, she was a woman of sense and of piety—Calvinistically tinged. Misfortune she took kindly; also her son's Catholicizing mission. This had not gone very far when she died, in the spring of 1836; the Oxford Movement being then only three years old. In the church at Littlemore which Newman built, with the funds of Oriel, he placed a tablet to the memory of his mother, who died just before its consecration; and a portrait of her remained upon his mantelpiece until the end.

The six children were equally divided as to sex; and the names of the three girls were Harriet, Jemima, and Mary. Harriet, the eldest, married in September, 1836, the Rev. Thomas Mozley, then already the brilliant Boswell of the future Cardinal. Before she died, Mrs. Thomas Mozley made two appearances as the author of children's stories, "The Fairy Bower" and "The Lost Brooch." Jemima married Mr. John Mozley, of Derby, in the spring of 1836; outlived her husband; and died, in Derby, about ten years before the death of the Cardinal. Yet another of the Mozley brothers, the Rev. Dr. James Mozley, had in 1832 described his future sisters-in-law in a letter home: "The Miss Newmans are very learned persons, deeply read in ecclesiastical history, and in all the old divines, both High Church and Puritanical. Notwithstanding—[Oh, why "notwithstanding"?]—they are very agreeable and unaffected." These two sisters were hero-worshippers, with John Henry for hero. They looked after his poor at Littlemore, and they gave him what he had the grace to thank, God for—

> A countless store
> Of eager smiles at home.

The family circle had been lessened so early as in 1828 by the death of the third and youngest girl. What Charlotte Brontë says in poignant words of her sister Emily may be said again: "Never in all her life had she lingered over any task that lay before her, and she did not linger now. (She sank rapidly. She made haste to leave us." In apparently perfect health one noon, Mary Newman by the next noon was gone. Pusey's thoughts turned affectionately to his friend in this hour of grief, almost panic. "Every consolation," he wrote, "which a brother can have he has most richly—her whole life having been a preparation for that hour." Other "Consolations in Bereavement" had Newman, and he thus expressed them:

> Death was full urgent with thee, sister dear,
> And startling in his speed ;

Brief pain, then languor till thy end came near—
    Such was the path decreed.
        The hurried road
To lead thy soul from earth to thine own God's abode.

Death wrought with thee, sweet maid, impatiently :
    Yet merciful the haste
That baffles sickness ;—dearest, thou didst die,
    Thou wast not made to taste
        Death's bitterness,
Decline's slow-wasting charm, or fever's fierce distress.

Death wrought in mystery ; both complaint and cure
    To human skill unknown :—
God put aside all means, to make us sure
    It was His deed alone ;
        Lest we should lay
Reproach on our poor selves that thou wast caught away.

Death came and went :—that so thy image might
    Our yearning hearts possess,
Associate with all pleasant thoughts and bright,
    With youth and loveliness ;
        Sorrow can claim,
Mary, nor lot nor part in thy soft soothing name.

Joy of sad hearts and light of downcast eyes !
    Dearest, thou art enshrined
In all thy fragrance in our memories ;
    For we must ever find
        Bare thought of thee
Freshen this weary life, while weary life shall be.

To both of his brothers, John Henry was able
to be a benefactor, in part a father : a nobly
common *rôle* which ought to give eldest brothers a
larger place among the heroes of romance. Francis

William, only four years younger, followed him to
school at Ealing, and then to Oxford, where he lived
for some time in lodgings, pursuing his studies with
as much docility as was in him under John Henry's
directions.   Already the difference of temperament
was marked, though in religion Frank was then an
Evangelical, John Henry not much more.   But,
even then, Frank thought him wanting in sympathy
with his Evangelical friends, so did not consult him
about his own difficulties.   But Frank himself!
A master of style, he made his words fit his strange
fancies about the Catholic religion ; they were as
arrows poisoned by his prejudices.   John Henry,
a little later, in what he thought a particularly
Apostolic mood, would not speak to Frank, whom
he had shortly before invoked in fraternal rhymes :

> Dear Frank, we both are summoned now,
>     As champions of the Lord ;
> Enrolled am I ; and shortly thou
>     Must buckle on the sword ;
> A high employ, nor lightly given,
> To serve as messengers of Heaven.

This season of syllogistic silence passed away.
The difference grew greater, but with a difference
—they agreed to differ.   They met from time to
time, in after-years, Frank visiting his brother at
Maryvale (where spirits were high) ; at Rednal ;
and in Birmingham.   Writing to Mr. Lilly in 1877,

Dr. Newman, as he then was, says : " The *Dublin* has a practice of always calling me *F.* Newman, whereas my brother is commonly distinguished from me by this initial, his name being Francis. I say this because, much as we love each other, neither would like to be mistaken for the other." Nor was there much fear. Francis William Newman, theist, vegetarian, anti-vaccinationist, to whom a monastery is even as a madhouse, and a nun a woman beside herself, had an utterance too distinct in its idiosyncrasy to be any but his own : and has it still—sole left of all his name.

It remains to speak of the least spoken-of member of the family, he of whom the Rev. Thomas Mozley ventures only : " There was also another brother, not without his share in the heritage of natural gifts." Charles Robert Newman, before he was out of his teens, decided that his brothers and sisters were too religious for him ; and he wrote to cousins, begging that he should no longer be thought of as a Newman : a vain desire, for only as such has he remembrance now. His mother was still alive, and she and his sisters tried to win him, but without success, from the life of self-elected loneliness. Never was a kindness denied him, however one-sided the kindnesses might be. Both his brothers, after they had been "cast off" by him, not he by them, as some have hinted, managed to put together funds for sending him to Bonn. But he came away without even offering himself for examination, a step he explained by saying that the judges would not grant him a degree because he had given offence by his treatment of faith and morals in an essay which ✓ they called *teterrima.* This was only one of a series of aids given by John Henry and by Francis, who, unlike in so much, resembled each other in their generous desires and actions towards their mother's youngest son. But in him they found, as one of them expresses it in a private letter, only "the closest representation of an ancient cynic philosopher this nineteenth century can afford." He had vicissitudes of fortune; and fortune was never much kinder than to cede him an ushership in a country school; a post it was not in his character to keep. For the last forty years of his life, which ended in 1884, he lived at Tenby; and there, two years before he died, he had a short visit from the Cardinal—at the very time when "Lead, kindly Light," was being sung at Christ Church round Pusey's open grave.

Born in Birchin Lane in the City of London in 1801, and spending his early years within almost a stone's throw of the Mansion House, John

Henry Newman did not go further afield than to Ealing for his first venture in the great world. From Dr. Nicholas's school he went straight to Trinity College, Oxford. Almost immediately afterwards the Newman family removed to Alton, where they stayed for two or three years. During that time John Henry spent his holidays there, delighting in White's "Natural History of Selborne," a few miles away. Other holidays in those earlier years of his Oxford life he spent with the Rev. Samuel Rickards, at Ulcombe in Kent, or at Stowlangtoft near Bury St. Edmunds. In 1827 he and his sisters paid a visit to Mr. Wilberforce, at Highwood, where one out of the four sons was already his pupil, and three were to be among his followers to Rome. Holidays were his season of verse-making. At Ulcombe he wrote "Nature and Art" in 1826, and "Snap-dragon" (a Trinity memory) in 1827. At Highwood he wrote "The Trance of Time."

After settling for a short time at Strand-on-the-Green, all who were left of the Newmans at home —the mother and two girls—went, in 1829, to a cottage at Horspath, to be near John Henry ; then to a cottage at Nuneham Courtney, offered to Newman by Dornford, a. Fellow of Oriel and a warm friend. " In the Midlands," says Thomas

Mozley, " it would have been set down as the habitation of a family of weavers or stockingers." But it had its associations. Rousseau had stayed in it; and Nuneham was supposed to be Goldsmith's Deserted Village. From Nuneham to Rosebank Cottage, Iffley, was no great move; and it was the last the family made.

In these wanderings during the earlier twenties of the century the Newmans had lived a while at Brighton. There John Henry wrote his " Paraphrase of Isaiah, chap. lxiv.," the second piece of his " Verses on Various Occasions," in 1821. Six years later and eight years later he visited Brighton again to see cousins, in one of whose albums he wrote verses on each visit. At Brighton, too, after his mother and sisters had left it for the neighbourhood of Oxford, Newman landed from the journey with Hurrell Froude to the south of Europe. The manuscript of " Lead, kindly Light," written on the voyage, was in his pocket ; and he was hurrying home, inspired by the conviction that he had " a work to do in England." He arrived just in time to hear Keble preach that sermon about " National Apostasy" on the Sunday in July, 1833, which began the Oxford Movement.

His life had been despaired of for a week in Sicily. He was in a high fever, and no medical

Lead, Kindly Light, amid the encircling gloom
       Lead Thou me on!
The night is dark, and I am far from home —
       Lead Thou me on!
Keep Thou my feet; I do not ask to see
The distant scene — one step enough for me.

I was not ever thus, nor prayed that Thou
       Shouldst lead me on.
I loved to choose and see my path, but now
       Lead Thou me on!
I loved the garish day, and, spite of fears,
Pride ruled my will: remember not past years.

So long Thy power hath blest me, sure it still
       Will lead me on,
O'er moor and fen, o'er crag and torrent, till
       The night is gone,
And with the morn those angel faces smile,
Which I have loved long since, and lost awhile.

          John Newman

help was at hand. A priest came and offered his services, which were declined. In his half-delirious caprice he got up and walked for some miles. Then he sank down exhausted, and was carried into a hovel, which a doctor chanced to pass, to whose care Newman owed his recovery. At Lyons he fell ill again ; his legs and ankles swelled —he thought with erysipelas. All this time—six weeks—his friends at home heard nothing of him, and were horribly anxious. When he landed in Brighton, having crossed from Dieppe, he still felt a little weakness lingering from the fever ; but he looked much better than when he set out, partly, perhaps, because his face was tanned by exposure to the sun.

To Brighton the Cardinal was destined to go again after yet another notable journey. This was on his return to England after visiting Rome in 1879 to receive his Cardinal's hat. On this journey, too, it had seemed that he must die ; but the time had not yet come, though he had done the work he felt he had to do when he set foot there nearly fifty years before. In the morning of the last. Sunday in June, 1879, accompanied by Father Neville, he went to the Church of St. John the Baptist, where he assisted at High Mass—for the first time in this country as a Cardinal. In

the afternoon he drove to the other Catholic
churches in the town, and visited the clergy
attached to them. The bells of Anglican steeples
rang out early in the morning, as only High
Churchmen make them ring, and all the day ; but
not invitingly for him, albeit he was, as the
*Guardian* candidly put it when he died, "the
founder of the Anglican Church as it now is."

# CHAPTER II.

## AT TRINITY AND ORIEL.

Degree—Scholar of Trinity—"Trinity had never been unkind to me "—A Trinity Sunday in after-life—A Trinity
friend—Fellow of Oriel—The first of Pusey and of
Keble—Diffidences—Ordination—First publicities—" I
began to be known "—The University pulpit—A group
of great listeners—Profound memories — Word-por-
traits—A prophet's chamber—Overheard prayers—A
neighbour at Oriel.

NEWMAN took his degree at Trinity College in
1820 ; and there he remained for three years longer
in the coveted position of Scholar.   For this home
of the first six years of his Oxford life he ever
retained a tender affection.   There he had the
dreams of his lay life ; there he moulded what was
afterwards matured.   When he left Oxford " for
good," as he himself phrased it, one of his friends
who came to Littlemore to say good-bye was Dr.
Ogle, who had been his private tutor at Trinity.
"In him," he says, "I took leave of my first
College, Trinity, which was so dear to me, and
which held in its foundation so many who had

been kind to me both when I was a boy, and all
through my Oxford life. Trinity had never been
unkind to me. There used to be much snap-dragon
growing on the walls opposite my freshman's rooms
there, and I had for years taken it as the emblem of
my own perpetual residence even unto death in my
University." At distant intervals during the next
thirty-two years a traveller to and from Birmingham looked from the railway carriage, with feelings
his fellows could not have divined, at the spires
of Oxford; but he did not revisit it until 1878·
Trinity attracted him there again, having elected
him in 1877 an Honorary Fellow. He was the
hero of cheering undergraduates ; and he attended
the College "gaudy" in the glare of limelight :
fêted for the first time in his already long life.

The feelings he all along entertained for his
old haunt had been expressed ten years earlier in
a letter, dated from Birmingham, Trinity Monday,
1868, and addressed to the Rev. Thomas Short, of
Trinity :—

MY DEAR SHORT,
        It is fifty years to-day since I was elected scholar
of Trinity. And, as you had so much to do with the election,
I consider you my first benefactor at Oxford. In memory of
it I have been saying Mass for you this morning. I should
not have ventured to write to tell you this ; but, happening
to mention it to William Neville, he said, " Do write and tell
him so, for I said Mass for him yesterday, being Trinity

Sunday." This letter will at least show the love we bear to
you and old Trinity amid all changes.  Take it as such, and
believe me to be, affectionately yours,

JOHN H. NEWMAN.

The Cardinal, during his visits to Oxford in
1878 and 1880, saw many old friends.  He called
on Mr. Short, who had then become blind, and
spent an hour with him.  He called also on Dr.
Pusey ; and on Mark Pattison, a guest at Littlemore, in 1843, altered out of all recognition.

After Trinity, Oriel seemed strange to Newman,
when, in 1823, it elected him to a Fellowship.
"During the first years of my residence at Oriel,"
he himself says, "though proud of my College, I
was not quite at home there.  I was very much
alone, and I used often to take my daily walk by
myself."  On one such occasion he met Dr.
Copleston, then Provost, who turned round, made
him a bow, and said : "Never less alone than when
alone."  At first he had no friend but Pusey ; and
even to Pusey, though Newman "could not fail to
revere a soul so devoted to the cause of religion, so
full of good works, so faithful in his affections," he
could not open his heart—then or afterwards.
Keble, too, was a Fellow of Oriel, and when Newman went to receive the congratulations of the
Fellows, he bore it all until Keble took his hand ;

and then, he says, " I felt so abashed and un-
worthy of the honour done me, that I seemed
desirous of quite sinking into the ground." But
Keble was not in residence ; and was shy of him,
so Newman thought, in consequence of the marks
he still bore of the Evangelical and Liberal schools.
Hurrell Froude, quoting the murderer who had
done one good thing in his life, boasted of himself
that he had brought Newman and Keble finally
" to understand each other " in 1828.

As time went on, things wonderfully changed.
By 1824 Newman took orders and was appointed
curate at St. Clément's ; he preached his first
University sermon ; became a tutor of his College,
and 'a public examiner ; and wrote one or two
essays which were well received. " I began to be
known." He had for his intimate friends Hurrell
Froude and Robert Isaac Wilberforce, afterwards
the fellow-Archdeacon of Manning in secession to
Rome. His hold on young men began. It was a
grip of goodness ; an attraction which was not of
earth—at a time when an attraction of the kind
was new and wonderful.

This influence was widely extended in 1828,
when he became Vicar of St. Mary the Virgin—a
post involving no change of residence. Though
primarily a parochial church, " gown " soon vied

C

with "town" in attendance. He had for his listeners the future clergy of the Church of England, of all schools, and not these only. In no other case quite so much expert and other testimony has been given to the influence of spoken words—as regards both the words themselves and the way they were spoken. That other great figure in the history of the revival of the Catholic Church in England forms a fitting first witness; for Cardinal Manning recalls even now, after a lapse of sixty years, being led captive by the "form and voice and penetrating words at Evensong in the University Church," where, having once seen and heard Newman, he "never willingly failed to be." Dean Stanley—no name follows Manning's as so great a contrast—agreed in this :

There are hardly any passages in English literature [he says] which have exceeded in beauty the description of music, in his University sermons; the description of the sorrows of human life in his sermon on the pool of Bethesda ; the description of Elijah on Mount Horeb ; or, again, in the discourses addressed to mixed congregations : " The Arrival of St. Peter as a Missionary in Rome ; " the description of Dives as the example of a self-indulgent voluptuary ; the account of the Agony in the Garden of Gethsemane, and of the growth in the belief in the Assumption of the Virgin Mary.

Among his listeners was one who was already studying the mechanism of oratory :

Now, Dr. Newman's manner in the pulpit [says Mr. Gladstone] was one about which, if you considered it in its separate parts, you would arrive at very unsatisfactory conclusions. There was not very much change in the inflexion of the voice ; action there was none. His sermons were read, and his eyes were always bent on his book, and all that, you will say, is against efficiency in preaching. Yes, but you take the man as a whole, and there was a stamp and a seal upon him ; there was a solemn sweetness and music in the tone ; there was a completeness in the figure, taken together with the tone and with the manner, which made even his delivery, such as I have described it, singularly attractive.

Principal Shairp put into words the thoughts of many hearts when he said : " On those calm Sunday afternoons he was heard preaching from the pulpit of St. Mary's, 'As if the angels and the dead were his audience.' That voice it was which thrilled young hearts—that living presence that drew to itself whatever there was in Oxford that was noble in purpose, or high and chivalrous in devotion." " No one," says Mr. James Anthony Froude, " who heard his sermons in those days can forget them : "

They were seldom directly theological. Newman, taking some Scripture character for a text, spoke to us about ourselves, our temptations, our experiences. His illustrations were inexhaustible. He seemed to be addressing the most secret consciousness of each of us—as the eyes of a portrait appear to look at every person in the room. They appeared to me to be the outcome of continued meditation upon his fellow-creatures and their position in the world, their awful responsibilities, the mystery of their nature, strangely mixed of good and evil, of strength and weakness. A tone, not of fear, but of infinite pity, ran through them all.

It was in St. Mary's that men learned how to bear great names greatly; like Lord Coleridge, who then founded the opinion he expressed in later years: " Raffaelle is said to have thanked ✓ God that he had lived in the days of Michael Angelo ; there are scores of men I know, there are hundreds and thousands I believe, who thank God that they have lived in the days of John Henry Newman." The voice is silent for ever now; but the printed words remain ; and these in bare type retain their hold. Mr. R. H. Hutton * confesses that the University sermons, and other works, have "fascinated" him ever since he was eighteen or nineteen ; and he adds : "I have often said that if it were ever my hard lot to suffer solitary confinement, and I were given my choice of books, and were limited to one or two, I should prefer some of Dr. Newman's to Shakspere himself."

A little incident, or a large one—who shall reckon?—brought Newman down from that pulpit in 1843—two years before his secession : the beginning of the great Renunciation. " It was," says

---

* " I have now for twenty years held him, as a journalist, to be a good friend of mine," the Cardinal wrote to me in 1884.

Principal Shairp, "as when to one kneeling by night, in the silence of some vast Cathedral, the great bell tolling solemnly overhead has suddenly gone still."

The young generation does not associate the name of Cardinal Newman with horses or vintages; but it is Mr. Froude, I think, who somewhere refers to him as the trusted wine-taster of his College; and to his love for horse exercise there are many allusions in Mr. Mozley's "Reminiscences." In his earlier Oriel days he rode a good deal. Besides taking his chance of the Oxford hacks, Newman had for some time a pretty, but dangerous animal, Klepper, brought over from Ireland by Lord Abercorn, then at Christchurch.

One little matter of self-imposed duty, arising out of a painful occasion, will [says Mr. Mozley] be remembered by all who ever accompanied Newman in a country walk. One morning Dornford asked him whether he was going to Littlemore that day, and whether on foot or horseback. He had to reply that he was riding there, when Dornford proposed to accompany him. This gentleman, having served two years in the Rifle Brigade in the Peninsular War, and being proud of his military character, was in the habit of cantering on the hard road, and had generally to do it alone. But Newman was in for it. In those days the first milestone between Oxford and Iffley was in a narrow, winding part of the road, between high banks, where nothing could be seen fifty yards ahead. Dornford and Newman heard the sound of a cart, and the latter detected its accelerated pace, but the impetuous "captain," as he loved to be styled, heeded it not.

It was the business of a cart to keep its own side. They
arrived within sight of the cart just in time to see the carter
jump down and be caught instantly between the wheel and the
milestone, falling dead on the spot. The shock on Dornford
was such that he was seriously ill for two months, and
hypochondriac for a much longer time. The result in Newman's case was a solemn vow that whenever he met a carter
driving without reins, or sitting on the shaft, he would make
him get down ; and this he never failed to do. Several years
after this sad affair, I was walking with him on the same
road. There came rattling on two newly-painted waggons,
drawn by splendid teams, that had evidently been taking
corn to market, and were now returning home without loads.
There were several men in the waggons, but no one on foot.
It occurred to me that as the waggoners were probably not
quite sober, it was only a choice of evils whether they were
on foot or in the waggons. But Newman had no choice ;
he was bound by his vow, and he compelled the men to come
down. We went on to Littlemore, were there for some time,
and then turned our faces homewards. Coming in sight of
the public-house at Littlemore, we saw the two show teams,
and something of a throng about them ; so we could not but
divine evil. It was too true. The waggoners had watched
us out of sight, and got into their waggons again. The
horses had run away on some alarm, one of the men had
jumped out, and had received fatal injuries.

Other examples of the Cardinal's habits of self-
discipline at this time are on record. He never
passed a day without writing a Latin sentence—
either a translation or an original composition—
before he had done his morning's work. Fre-
quently, when on the point of leaving his room for
an afternoon walk, he has asked a friend to stay
a minute or two while he was writing his daily

sentence. Then, too, he wrote and laid by a complete history of every serious question in which he was concerned, such as that of the College tuition. He did the same with every book he read and every subject he inquired into. He drew up a summary or an analysis of the matter, or of his own views upon it. Mr. Mozley's further outlining of his brother-in-law at this period tallies with the " Sketch from St. Mary's "—from the pencil of an undergraduate :—

Newman did not carry his head aloft or make the best use of his height. He did not stoop, but he had a slight bend forwards, owing perhaps to the rapidity of his movements, and to his always talking while he was walking. His gait was that of a man upon serious business bent, and not on a promenade. There was no pride in his port or defiance in his eye. Though it was impossible to see him without interest and something more, he disappointed those who had known him only by name. They who saw for the first time the man whom some warm admirer had described in terms above common eulogy, found him so little like the great Oxford don or future pillar of the Church, that they said he might pass for a Wesleyan minister. John Wesley must have been a much more imposing figure. Robust and ruddy sons of the Church looked on him with condescending pity as a poor fellow whose excessive sympathy, restless energy, and general unfitness for this practical world would soon wreck him. Thin, pale, and with large lustrous eyes ever piercing through this vale of men and things, he hardly seemed made for this world. Canon Bull meeting him one day in the Parks, after hearing he had been unwell, entreated him to spare what fibre he had for a useful career. " No ordinary frame can stand long such work as yours." His dress—it became almost the badge of his followers—was the long-tailed coat, not always very new. There is a strange tendency in religious schools to express themselves in outward forms, often from the merest accident. Newman, however, never studied his "get up," or even thought of it. He had other uses for his income which in these days would have been thought poverty. It became the fashion of the party to despise solemnity of manner and stateliness of gait. Newman walked quick, and, with a congenial companion, talked incessantly. George Ryder said of him that when his mouth was shut it looked as if it never could open; and when it was open it looked as if it never could shut. Yet he was never so busy or so preoccupied but that he had always upon him a burden of conscientious duties to be attended to, calls of civility or kindness, promises to be fulfilled, bits of thoughtfulness to be carried out, rules of his own to be attended to.

Mr. J. A. Froude's description is, perhaps, misleadingly picturesque :—

He was above middle height, slight and spare. His head was large, his face remarkably like that of Julius Cæsar. The forehead, the shape of the ears and nose, were almost the same. The lines of the mouth were very peculiar, and I should say exactly the same. In both men there was an original force of character, which refused to be moulded by circumstances, which was to make its own way, and become a power in the world ; a clearness of intellectual perception, a disdain for conventionalities, a temper imperious and wilful, but along with it a most attaching gentleness, sweetness, singleness of heart and purpose. Both were formed by Nature to command others ; both had the faculty of attracting to themselves the passionate devotion of their friends and followers.

Newman's rooms at Oriel, on the first floor near

the chapel, communicated with what was no better than a large closet, overlighted with an immense bay-window over the chapel door. It had been a lumber-room ; but, says Mozley, " Newman fitted it up as a prophet's chamber, and there, night after night, in the Long Vacation of 1835, offered up prayers for himself and the Church. Returning to College late one night I found that, even in the gateway, I could not only hear the voice of prayer, but could even distinguish words. The result was, Newman contented himself with a less poetical oratory." Strangers coming daily to Oxford, and seeking out the abode of the man who was "moving the Church of England to its foundations," were surprised to find him in simple undergraduate's lodgings. In the rooms above lived William Froude, Hurrell's younger brother, who was to be Brunel's helper in laying out the Bristol and Exeter Railway, and who was to make for himself a more difficult spiritual way to Rome. While Newman was praying, William Froude was making laughing gas and staining his window-sills with sulphuric acid. From 1837 to 1840, Mozley records: " Newman had no College office or work, and was seldom seen in Hall ; but he gave receptions every Tuesday evening in the Common Room, largely attended by both College and out-College men."

Though he was to take the second step in the great Renunciation, and to leave the University and the city, he did not resign his Fellowship until the fateful October of 1845.

# CHAPTER III.

## LITTLEMORE.

Search after seclusion—Cloister, cells, and crucifix—Resolution as to his position—Disciples—Hard fasting—A significant visit—The first to go—Curiosity, and Newman's resentment of it—Father Dominic receives Newman—A first and last Mass—A Jesuit's strange offer—Primitive confession—Father Newsham's laughter—Final farewells.

NEWMAN had too many visitors in Oriel to be able to give time and thought to serious religious studies and exercises ; so he withdrew to Littlemore, which lies two or three miles to the south of Oxford, towards London. He had always loved the place, and it had the tradition of being the healthiest spot thereabout. The parish was a hamlet of St. Mary the Virgin ; and for many years Newman walked from Oxford to Littlemore two or three times a week. Since he had built a little church there, the sound of the stonemason's hammer had not been heard, and he could find

nothing better for his new residence than a dis-
used range of stabling at the corner of two roads.

Nothing could be more unpromising ; but Newman said it was enough ; and his handy man was
there to help in the work of reconstruction—
Thomas Mozley, a master-builder, too, of words,
whose " Reminiscences " have again and again
helped me in the patchwork of these temporary
memoirs. Newman made known his needs. There
must be a library, some " cells," and a cloister—the
chapel was to be for future consideration. The
library was to be the common workroom ; and
each cell was to contain a sitting-room, say twelve
feet by nine feet, a bedroom six feet by six feet ;
the height of both to be nine or ten feet. Newman
bought nine acres which he proposed to plant with
firs, and on which he could build, bit by bit, as
money came and men. He expressed only one
sentimental wish to the reconstructor—that he
might be able to see from his own cell window the
ruins of the Mynchery—a convent dating from
Saxon times, inhabited of old by generations of
Benedictine Nuns, and dedicated to " Our Lady of
Littlemore." Newman's decision as he paced the
cloister, or knelt before the crucifix (for he had
ceased to be superstitiously afraid of crucifixes), or
studied the Fathers, now was: that he could go on

in the University pulpit only on condition that he was allowed to hold by the Catholic interpretation of the Anglican Articles set forth in " Tract XC." ; but that he would relapse into lay life in the Church of England rather than join the Church of Rome "while she suffered honours to be paid to the Blessed Virgin and the Saints, which I thought in my conscience to be incompatible with the Supreme, Incommunicable Glory of the One Infinite and Eternal ;"* that he desired a union between the Churches, on conditions ; that Littlemore was, as he called it, his *Torres Vedras,* and that he and his followers might advance again within the Anglican Church, as they had been forced to retire ; and, finally, that he must keep back with all his might intending seceders to Rome. Everything indicated that he came to the village to stay—not to make it, as it turned out to be, his home of only five or six years' duration.

When all was done, the place still looked outside

---

* Looking back to those days, after years of experience as a Catholic, he says : "Only this I know full well now, and did not know then, that the Catholic Church allows no image of any sort, material or immaterial, no dogmatic symbol, no rite, no sacrament, no Saint, not even the Blessed Virgin herself, to come between the soul and its Creator. It is face to face, *solus cum solo,* in all matters between man and his God. He alone creates ; He alone has redeemed ; before His awful eyes we go in death, and in the vision of Him is our eternal beatitude."

what it had always been—a range of stabling. But these were not the times for "externals;" and the cells were soon filled with men all in deadly earnest about "the interior life." "They were most of them," says Newman, "keenly religious men, with a true concern for their souls as the first matter of all, with a great zeal for me, but. giving little certainty at the time as to which way they would ultimately turn. Some, in the event, have remained firm to Anglicanism, some have become Catholics, and some have found a refuge in Liberalism." Of the latter, one name comes to mind on the moment—that of Mark Pattison. Pattison had his habitation in a sort of Community-house established on Apostolic principles by Pusey in Oxford itself; and he was a guest, not a resident, when he stayed at Littlemore. What attracted the future Rector of Lincoln College to Tractarianism was "the interest it excited in the young in all religious practices and exercises, and in many religious questions which had been matters of indifference." * Mark Pattison

---

* Newman somewhere says that his old friends were distressed to see him surrounded in the early 'forties by "younger men of a cast of mind in no small degree uncongenial to my own." Some of this was raw material, certainly; and so remained. In after-life Mark Pattison wrote: "I am astonished to see what hours I wasted (!) over religious books at a time when I ought to have been devoting every moment to preparation for the Oriel Examination." On a

kept a diary during a fortnight's visit to Newman
at the close of September, 1843, and these are
some of the entries, showing what manner of life
the men of Littlemore led :—

Newman kinder, but not perfectly so.* Vespers at eight.
Compline at nine. How low, mean, selfish, my mind has
been to-day; all my good deeds vanished; grovelling, sensual,
animalist ; I am not, indeed, worthy to come under this roof !
Sunday, October 1st.—St. John called me at 5.30, and at
six went to Matins, which, with half Lauds and Prime, takes
about an hour and a half; afterwards returned to my room
and prayed, with some effect, I think. Tierce at nine, and
at eleven to church—communion. More attentive and devout
than I have been for some time ; thirty-seven communicants.

---

par with this are the reasons he gives for not joining the Catholic
Church : "I must have been enveloped in the catastrophe of 1845,
as were so many of those with whom I lived, but for two saving
circumstances. One of these was my devotion to study. In 1843
Radford offered me a tutorship of the College. My classics had got
sadly rusty. I immediately set resolutely to work and made good
my lost ground. I think it was chiefly owing to this that when the
crash came in 1845 I did not follow Newman." Later on, in his
"Memoirs," Mark Pattison, feeling perhaps that everything still
remained to be said on this subject, gives another version. He
says: "In dealing with the students I soon became aware that I
was the possessor of a magnetic influence, which soon gave me a
moral ascendancy in the College. In this fact, which was very
slowly making itself felt, lies the true secret of my not having
followed Newman." When some one compiles—O strangest collection of inadequacies !—a volume of men's "Reasons why I did *not*
join the Church of Rome," Mark Pattison's will still remain, with
Keble's, among the most perplexing.

* Poor Mark Pattison, in his self-torturing sensitiveness, had
supposed, "up to 1838 the only sentiment Newman can have entertained towards me was one of antipathy."

Returned and had breakfast. Had some discomfort at waiting for food so long. Walked up and down with St. John in the garden ; Newman afterwards joined us ; and at three to church ; then Nones ; walked in the garden till dinner—interesting talk. Some unknown benefactor sent a goose. Talk of some Rosminian Nuns coming to England ;* though an Order, and under the three vows, they do not renounce possessions in the world. They aim to embrace the whole Church. The Jesuits always and everywhere opposed and despised ; St. Ignatius prayed for this ; Wiseman opposed the Jesuits at Rome, and does so here ; proof of his sincerity. Vespers at eight, Compline at nine. Very sleepy, and went to bed at ten.

October 3rd.—Lockhart's mother much distressed. Probably at the separation, more than at the conversion, which she must have expected some time.

October 4th.—N—— mentioned to me having just received the account of a lady who, having in conversation declared she thought the Church of Rome the true Church, had been refused the Communion by her minister, he telling her in so many words to go to Rome.

October 5th.—Coffin came to-day to stay. How uncomfortable have I made myself all this evening by a childish fancy that once got into my head—a weak jealousy of N——'s good opinion ! Oh ! my God, take from me this petty pride ! Coffin more subdued and less thoughtless than usual.

This particular way of introducing the name of Coffin will perhaps surprise those afterwards acquainted with the ascetic Provincial of the English Redemptorists, who took on himself, when at the end of his life, the burden of the Bishopric of

---

* The future Rosminian, Father Lockhart, was *not* at the dinner-table. He had gone on pilgrimage to the shrines of St. Gilbert of Sempringham ; and on the journey he joined the Catholic Church.

Southwark. Other men of Littlemore, belonging to the group who became Catholics, were Frederick S. Bowles, now Chaplain to the Dominican Nuns at Harrow ; John B. Dalgairns, afterwards a London Oratorian, a man of whom Mozley says, " I feel sure he might have taken his place among the most popular and instructive writers of the age, and become a household word in England ; " "dear Ambrose St. John," the "link between the old life and the new," who lived with Newman as a fellow-priest at the Birmingham Oratory, and now lies with him in one grave at Rednal ; Albany Christie, now a Jesuit, who was studying medicine in London with as many interludes at Littlemore as he could get ; Bridges, of Merton, whose brother George, and his cousin Matthew, became Catholics too ; Richard Stanton, now an Oratorian in London ; and Lockhart, the first to go.

If Lockhart's mother was distressed,[*] his master was so too. Speaking of his young men, and of this young man, Newman said : " Their friends besought me to quiet them if I could. Some of them came to live with me at Littlemore. They were laymen or in the place of laymen. I kept some of them back for several years from being received into the Catholic Church. The

---

[*] She herself became a Catholic shortly afterwards.

immediate cause of my resigning St. Mary's was the unexpected conversion of one of them." This was Lockhart; who, after confessing to Newman one day, asked: "But are you sure you have the power of absolution?" "Why will you ask me that question?" replied Newman—"ask Pusey." To Pusey the Littlemorians always supposed that Newman himself went; so that Pusey could now at least aver that he gave that amount of proof of his belief in the absolving power of the Anglican clergy. But Lockhart did not trouble Pusey with his question. He went to Father Gentili, whom he had lately met with the De Lisles at Ward's rooms in Oxford; and at the end of a three days' retreat was a Catholic and a Postulant with the Rosminians. Rosmini's "Maxims of Perfection" had been given to him four years earlier by a friend—now Sir William White, our Ambassador at Constantinople; and one of the counsels on which he opened in a moment of hesitation decided him that his duty was to submit there and then to the Catholic Church, despite the promise Newman had extorted from him to linger for three years longer. Father Lockhart, looking back at those days, said in a lecture delivered in St. Etheldreda's, Ely Place, just after Newman's death:

In speaking of Cardinal Newman and his work, he should

necessarily speak of himself, though he spoke of himself only
as a type of the ordinary young Oxford man who came fifty
years ago under the great Cardinal's influence. To put into
one sentence what struck him as the character of his whole
teaching and influence, it was to make them use their
reasoning powers, to seek after the last satisfactory reason
one could reach of everything, and this led them to the last
reason of all, and they formed a religious personal belief in
God the Creator, our Lord and Master. This was the first
thing that Newman did for those young men under his care.
He rooted in their hearts and minds a personal conviction
of the living God.' And he for one could say he never had
had that feeling of God before he was brought into contact
with Cardinal Newman. Who that had experience of it
could forget Newman's majestic countenance?—the meekness,
the humility, the purity of a virgin heart "in work and will,"
as the poet says, a purity that was expressed in his eyes, his
kindness, the sweetness of his voice, his winning smile, his
caressing way, which had in it nothing of softness, but which
you felt was a communication to you of strength from a
strong soul—a thing to be felt in order to be realised. It
was when Newman read the Scriptures from the lectern in
St. Mary's Church at Oxford that one felt more than ever
that his words were those of a seer who saw God and the
things of God. Many men were impressive readers, but
they did not reach the soul. They played on the senses and
imagination, they were good actors, they did not forget themselves, and one did not forget them. But Newman had the
power of so impressing the soul as to efface himself; you
thought only of the majestic soul that saw God. It was God
speaking to you as He speaks to you through creation ; but
in a deeper way, by the articulate voice of man made to the
image of God and raised to His likeness by grace, com-
municating to your intelligence and sense and imagination,
by words which were the signs of ideas, a transcript of the
work and private thoughts that were in God. . . . Hearing
of Newman's intention to open a place at Littlemore he

volunteered to join him, and was accepted. He was one of the first inmates of that home. Newman rooted theism most deeply in their souls, and from that they were led on to the practice of submission and of that religion which they doubted not had come from God, for they had no doubt whatever that the Church of England was a part of that world-wide religious society which Christ had established in the beginning, and which He sent down His Apostles to establish in every land. It was only after beginning to put, in practice what Newman had taught them—to go into the last reason of things, which they did step by step, in many cases quite independently of their teacher, because he became a Catholic two years before Newman—that they arrived at that conclusion which he himself reached a little later. Newman was much hurt for his leaving him. But the first step that Newman took after he had become a Catholic was to pay him a visit at the College at which he was then studying. He need not say how happy that day was when he found himself and his old friend once more in the same communion.

After preaching his last sermon as an Anglican in September, 1843, Newman remained two years longer at Littlemore—making sure that he was not doing anything in a hurry. "It is," he says, "because the Bishops still go on charging against me, though I have quite given up: it is that secret misgiving of heart which tells me that they do well, for I have neither lot nor part with them; this it is which weighs me down." And he adds a smaller grief, but to him a real grievance: "I cannot walk into or out of my house, but curious eyes are upon me. Why will you not let me die

in peace? Wounded brutes creep into some hole
to die in, and no one grudges it them. Let me
alone, I shall not trouble you long." One day,
when he entered the house, he found a flight of
undergraduates inside. Heads of houses, as
mounted patrols, walked their horses round the
poor cottages; Doctors of Divinity dived into the
recesses of that private tenement uninvited. When
the Warden of Wadham, a flourishing Evangelical,
knocked one day at the door, Newman opened it
himself :—nothing so human as a housemaid entered
the "monastery," where the inmates took the duty
of door-opening for a week by turns. "May I see
the monastery?" insinuated the visitor. "We
have no monasteries here," replied Newman, and
closed the door in his face—less than civil! Then
the newspapers had their paragraphs, inviting
episcopal attention. So the Bishop of Oxford
writes, a little timidly, to ask what it all means :—
Is there really an intention to found—he can
hardly bring himself to write the naughty word
Archdeacon Farrar and all of them have now so
glibly at the tongue's end—an Anglican monastery? Newman replies :

For many years, at least thirteen, I have wished to give
myself to a life of greater religious regularity than I have
hitherto led ; but it is very unpleasant to confess such a wish

even to my Bishop. I feel it very cruel, though the parties in fault do not know what they are doing, that very sacred matters between me and my conscience are made a matter of public talk. As to the quotation from the newspaper, your Lordship will perceive that "no monastery is in process of erection ;" there is no " chapel," no " refectory," hardly a dining-room or parlour. The "cloisters" are my shed connecting the cottages. I do not understand what "cells of dormitories" means. Of course, I can repeat your Lordship's words that " I am not attempting a revival of the Monastic Orders, in anything approaching the Romanist sense of the term."

Rumours flew about ; and it was whispered that he "was already in the service of the enemy"— had already been received into the Catholic Church. On the other hand, among Catholics there were murmurs—could he know so much, and yet remain in good faith? What a rebuke it seemed when the Bishop of Clifton recalled rash judgments in the presence of the coffin containing all that was mortal of this immortal man! That the resignation of St. Mary's gave him a new sense of freedom is implied by Newman in the letter he wrote in April, 1845, to Cardinal Wiseman, then Vicar-Apostolic, who had accused him of past coldness in his conduct towards him :

I was at that time in charge of a ministerial office in the English Church, with persons entrusted to me, and a Bishop to obey ; how could I write otherwise than I did without violating sacred obligations? . . . If you knew me, you would acquit me, I think, of having ever felt towards your

Lordship in an unfriendly spirit, or ever having had a shadow on my mind of what might be called controversial rivalry, or desire of getting the better, or fear lest the world should think I had got the worst, or irritation of any kind. And now in like manner, pray believe, though I cannot explain it to you, that I am encompassed with responsibilities so great and so various as utterly to overcome me unless I have mercy from Him Who, all through my life, has sustained and guided me, and to Whom I can now submit myself, though men of all parties are thinking evil of me.

The story of the life at Littlemore has never yet been entirely told ; and it would be impossible to glean from Newman's scanty allusions in the " Apologia," or even from his letter to the Bishop, any idea of its primitive austerities and observances. I tell these as they are told to me by Littlemore men. Lent was a season of real penance for the inmates of the monastery. They had nothing to eat each day till five, and then the solitary meal was of salt fish. No wonder Dr. Wootten, the Tractarian doctor, told them they must all die in a few years if things went on so ; and no wonder Dalgairns had a serious illness ; after which re-laxations were made. A breakfast of bread and butter and tea was taken at noon, the monks standing up at a board—a real board, erected in the improvised refectory, and called in undertones by some naturally fastidious ones a " trough." The " chapel " was hardly more pretentious than

the dining-room.   At one end stood a large crucifix, bought at Lima by Mr. Crawley, a Spanish
merchant living in Littlemore.   It was what was
called "very pronounced"—with the all but
barbaric realism of Spanish religious art.   A table
supported the base; and on the table were two
candles lighted at prayer-time by Newman himself
—and necessary—for Newman had veiled the
window and walls with his favourite red hangings.
Of an altar there was no pretence; the village
church at Littlemore being Newman's own during
the first years of his residence there.   A board ran
up the centre of the chapel, and in a row on either
side stood the disciples for the recitation of Divine
Office; "the Vicar," as his disciples called him,
standing by himself a little apart.   The days and
hours of the Catholic Church were duly kept; and
the only alteration made in the Office was that
Saints were invoked with a modification of Newman's making—the "*Ora* pro nobis" being changed
in recitation to "*Oret.*"   At Christmas and Easter
some white silk was placed behind the crucifix,
upon the background of red hangings [those red
hangings—almost mauve—reappear at Maryvale.
and at Edgbaston—horrors!], a symbol and pro-
clamation of Divine grace.

Among the visitors to Littlemore, a year before

*the* visit, was Father Dominic himself. He came, passing through Oxford, and presented himself at Newman's door as one watching with keen interest Anglican development in Christian doctrine. " A *little more* grace," he said, and then the consummation :—an Italian, new to the English language, must be ceded the pleasure of the pun. Newman took him to Littlemore Church ; and there the Father fell on his knees—doubtless to pray for the happy issue of these strange workings of Divine grace in the heart of Oxford—in the hearts of the very flower of the University which Protestantism had appropriated, and fenced in, and planted about. *

If, on the night of October 8th, 1845, any dons or proctors were prying round the "monastery " (even Newman could not persist in calling it the " parsonage-house " after he had ceased to be the parson), they must have seen a strange sight—a monk indeed ! Father Dominic, the Passionist,

---

* A dear friend of mine, an Irish priest, told me he felt a little strange when, years afterwards, he found himself impelled to kneel in the same place. Father Dawson, O.M.I., did not know he was but doing what Father Dominic had done. Nor did Mr. F. W. Grey, the grandson given by the great Lord Grey to the Faith, who writes : " Silently we knelt in the deserted temple and prayed that its Lord and Master, banished for three hundred years, might quickly return to it again, and then rose and continued our pilgrimage."

was that night to find the consummation of those
hopes he had held almost from the days when he
watched his sheep on the Apennines : those hopes
that he might get to Northern Europe and to
Protestantism, and preach the full Gospel of Christ.
The years passed ; and the shepherd lad found
himself a priest, and was sent to England—and to ·
Aston in Staffordshire. And now Dalgairns, who
had already been received by Father Dominic at
Aston, and who had returned to find "the Vicar"
at the last gasp of Anglicanism, and Ambrose St.
John also reconciled to the Church by Monsignor
Brindle at Prior Park, suggested that the Passionist
should again visit Littlemore. He came, dripping
wet from his journey through torrents of rain.
Newman knelt before him. The Father, bade the
neophyte rise, " conscious," says one of his friends,
"of a great miracle of grace." Mr. Oakeley, one
of Newman's young disciples, who subsequently
exchanged the Anglican ministry for the Catholic
priesthood, says :

It was a memorable day, that 9th of October, 1845. The
rain came down in torrents, bringing with it the first heavy
instalment of autumn's sere and yellow leaves. The wind,
like a spent giant, howled forth the expiring notes of its
equinoctial fury. The superstitious might have said that the
very elements were on the side of Anglicanism—so copiously
did they weep, so piteously bemoan, the approaching de-

parture of its great representative. The bell which swung visibly in the turret of the little Gothic church at Littlemore gave that day the usual notice of morning and afternoon prayers ; but it came to the ear in that buoyant, bouncing tone which is usual in a high wind, and sounded like a knell rather than a summons. The monastery was more than usually sombre and still. Egress and ingress there were none that day ; for it had been given out, among friends. accustomed to visit there, that Mr. Newman "wished to remain quiet." One of these friends, who resided in the neighbourhood, had been used to attend the evening "office" in the oratory of the house, but he was forbidden to come "for two or three days, for reasons which would be explained later." The ninth of the month passed off without producing any satisfaction to the general curiosity. All that transpired was that a remarkable-looking man, evidently a foreigner, and shabbily dressed in black, had asked his way to Mr. Newman's on the day but one before ; and the rumour was that he was a Catholic priest. In the course of a day or two the friend before mentioned was re-admitted to the evening office, and found that a change had come over it. The Latin was pronounced for the first time in the Roman way, and the antiphons of Our Lady, which up to that day had always been omitted, came out in their proper place. The friend in question would have asked the reason of these changes, but it was forbidden to speak to any of the Community after night-prayers. Very soon the mystery was cleared up by Mr. Newman and his companions appearing at Mass in the public chapel at Oxford.

Father Dominic, after spending some hours in Newman's "cell," visited Bowles and Stanton. His bow to the Pietà—a German coloured print— as he entered Bowles's room, was a part of his pious simplicity :—Newman said of him he had met no one in whom so much simplicity combined with so much shrewdness ; a common Italian type which he must have encountered often enough afterwards. "My dear brother," Father Dominic began to Bowles, "I am surprised that you should dwell in a Church which has no ideas." What followed is hardly remembered now ; but need for controversy there was none. The watering and the planting and the grafting (a great deal of that) had been done : now came the harvest. Stanton was a young clergyman, formerly of Brasenose College, and a Hulme Exhibitioner, who had resigned his benefice and come to Littlemore. These three, "the Vicar" and the two disciples, entered the curious chapel on Thursday afternoon, October 9th, 1845, and stood in a line together. Function there was none ; and Ritualism hid her face. The bowl of Baptism was of domestic, not of ecclesiastical pattern ; and all else was of a tale.

Then Father Dominic gave a little address, saying his *Nunc Dimittis*. Dalgairns and St. John went into Oxford, to the primitive Catholic chapel —St. Clement's—and borrowed from the old priest, Father Newsham, an altar-stone and vestments, so that Father Dominic might say Mass the next morning—the first and only time at Littlemore.

At that Mass the neophytes received their first
Communion. The fervour of Father Dominic,
when he made his thanksgiving, greatly impressed
the converts, who had not been accustomed in
Anglicanism to see so much emotion in prayer.
One little incident may be recorded as almost
comic. On the evening before their reception into
the Church, Father Dominic went into the chapel
with the catechumens, and recited Office with
them. But when they came to the record of how
St. Denis, after his martyrdom, put his head under
his arm and walked about, Father Dominic cried
"stop," and skipped it over. He thought such
legends might be a difficulty to beginners; but he
did not know his men; for who was more familiar
with miracles and the authority assigned to them
than the author of those Essays which had made
Macaulay exclaim, "The times require a Middleton"? In truth, the neophytes were a little
scandalized at *him*, and not at all at it.*

Father Dominic left at the end of a three days'

* Four years later, when the Oratorian Series of Saints' Lives
began to be published, the Convert Editors found themselves dis-
countenanced in their love of legend by old Catholics; and the
series was temporarily stopped by Newman after it had been
accused, in *Dolman's Magazine*, of reducing Hagiology to a string
of "unmeaning puerilities." Newman himself hinted afterwards
that he had been led into extravagances by "younger men."

visit. As he went back to Oxford he must have recalled a passage in the life of the Founder of the Passionists—St. Paul of the Cross. It tells how he fell into a trance, at the end of which he was asked what vision he had seen, and answered: "O the wonderful works of my children in England!" Confessor and penitent met once again at Maryvale. But the Passionist had done his work. In 1849, he was travelling by rail with one companion, when his mortal illness seized him, and he died upon the platform of Reading Station, blessing England with his latest breath. By some deplorable chance the people who were near, and who might have helped him, feared some infection, and held aloof from him and refused him shelter. Thus died this lover of our country, the humble apostle who reconciled to the Catholic Church him whom her Head afterwards called "the light of England."

For four months after his conversion Newman remained at Littlemore. It was a strange period. The converts went down daily to Oxford to Mass —great curiosities! They took the path through the fields to escape the public gaze. There is a fine church in Oxford now, and there are Jesuits to man it. But the old St. Clement's was almost comic in its insufficiencies. One announcement

made on Sunday was : " Confessions will be heard
on Saturday afternoon in the arbour." The arbour
in some way communicated with the schoolroom ;
and a penitent of the party repairing thither, feeling
all the first shyness of a never anything but shy
proceeding, found an unexpected embarrassment.
Just as the critical moment came, he heard the
young barbarians stop their play to listen. " Hush,"
said the leader, " he's going to begin." There was
at least the precedent of the early Church, when
Confession was publicly made. Father Newsham
walked over to Littlemore ; and during his call was
perpetually breaking out into ripples of laughter.
Newman was a little sore about it. "What did he
find so funny about us ?" he asked, when the visitor
went. The reassuring truth leaked out : the good
priest was so overjoyed—he could not contain
himself. At last grace had done its work—and he
had as his parishioner at St. Clement's the great
Mr. Newman of St. Mary's. Other visitors came
—among them the Provincial of the Jesuits, with
a proposition—astonishing ! The Society had a
work in hand, and would the converts help in it ?—
an apostolate in Timbuctoo. Then came partings,
the saddest that ever voluntarily were ; with Mr.
Pattison and Mr. Lewis, one of whom followed
Newman to Rome at leisure, and Mr. Church,

afterwards Dean of St. Paul's. "You may think how lonely I am. We are leaving Littlemore, and it is like going on the open sea." *

Father Dawson, during a visit from Ireland to England in 1890, made a pilgrimage to the death-bed of Newman's Anglicanism. Writing of it as it now is, he says in a letter to me: "Yes! that· was it—just a little row of one-storey cottages on the side of the village street, and a similar row, joined to it at right angles, running into a lane. The cottages are now in reality separate cottages ; but one grave old lady most politely showed me what (as she understood) had been the chapel, the refectory, and the dormitory. It looked, indeed, a place of plain · living. 'Remember him myself? Oh yes! I can remember Mr. Newman *very* well indeed—hearing him preach in the church, and seeing him in the school when I was a little girl. He *was* kind to us, sir, when he used to come into the school; we were all so fond of him. Ah! what a pity, sir, he ever left us!' On that point

---

* In the "Apologia," written nearly twenty years later, the Cardinal speaks of spending the last two days at Littlemore "simply by myself"—a slip of memory. Father Bowles was there till the end ; and into his room Newman came each evening, and fell asleep in his chair, worn out with the day's packing. On their last night in Oxford, Newman slept "at my dear friend's, Mr. Johnson's, at the Observatory," as also did Father Bowles.

I did not feel willing to dwell, or even to find out for certain whether my venerable hostess meant by ' leaving us ' anything besides leaving the village of Littlemore."

# CHAPTER IV.

### MARYVALE, ROME, COTTON HALL, AND ALCESTER STREET, BIRMINGHAM.

Gives up the idea of a lay life—Confirmed at Oscott—Goes
   to Maryvale—Two places in a coach and five vans of
   books—Studies and Ordination in Rome—"We are to
   be Oratorians "—Return to Maryvale—Is joined by
   Faber—Goes to Cotton Hall—A call to London—The
   choice of Birmingham—The Achilli trial—The libel
   itself—A prisoner of a minute—A house in a slum—
   Cholera duty at Bilston—"Mostly poor and Irish "—
   Literary and other labour not in vain in the Lord.

AT first Newman had talked of "secular employ-
ment ;" but Bishop Wiseman knew better. The
neophyte came to Oscott, near Birmingham, to be
confirmed by the Bishop on November 1st, 1845 ;
together with Oakeley, who had been received into
the Church by Father Newsham at Oxford ; and
Mr. Walker, a great friend of Stanton, and, like him,
a young ex-clergyman, late of Brasenose, and afterwards a Catholic priest.   While at Oscott, Newman
was taken by Wiseman to see a building, then

used as a boys' school, near to the College and
belonging to it. "Bring your friends here," said
Wiseman, "and carry on your studies for the
priesthood, with the help of our professors at
Oscott." Newman accepted the house, and called
it "Maryvale." Thither he went, accompanied by
Bowles, inside the coach from Oxford, on Monday,
February 23rd, 1846. Stanton and St. John had
gone before to prepare the house, they having
cleverness in such arrangements; and Newman's
own furniture and books—especially books—were
on the road in five enormous vans.

After a few months at Maryvale, Newman went
to Rome, pausing here and there upon the way,
The *Univers* of September 20th, 1846, published
the following letter from Langres :—

The presence of the Rev. J. H. Newman in our city has
excited no less interest than it did at Paris. His simplicity
and modesty charmed every one who had the advantage of
an admission to his presence. Our venerable Bishop received him with the affection and cordiality of a brother.
Forty or fifty members of our clerical body had the honour
of being presented to him whose eloquent words affected
so lately the studious youth of the principal University of
England. The marks of sympathy of which this learned
writer was the object have spoken to him of the happiness
which Catholics experience in counting him among their
brethren. What admirable men are these Oxford converts !
God has not without purpose chosen instruments so fitted to
accomplish His great designs. Mr. Newman was accom-

panied by the Rev. Ambrose St. John, who, also, has been
admitted to Minor Orders, and repairs to Rome to receive
the priesthood. The second companion of Mr. Newman is
the Rev. Robert Aston Coffin. Mr. Coffin does not proceed
to Rome with his two friends, but returns to England. Mr.
Newman and Mr. St. John go from Langres to Besançon.
They will travel through Switzerland to Milan, where they
remain till they have learnt Italian* before proceeding to
Rome. Mr. Dalgairns, who is completing his theological.
studies at Langres, hopes to return to England next year,
where he will await the return from Rome of his friend and
instructor.

Of the Archbishop of Besançon, Newman wrote :
" He has the reputation and the carriage of a very
saintly man." " What you want in England is a
strong Bishop," said the Prelate ; and Newman,
who thought things went a little too easily, agreed.
The arrival in Rome is recorded by the Roman
correspondent of the *Daily News*, which had
started, under Dickens's editorship, on the very
day following Newman's departure from Oxford—
an event it did not think worth a mention. The
Roman correspondent—no other than " Father
Prout "—says :

On the evening of October 28th Mr. Newman, accompanied by Mr. Ambrose St. John, entered the Eternal City.

---

* Newman had learnt some Italian before his tour with Hurrell
Froude in 1833, but it was obliterated from his memory during his
fever in Sicily ; and he afterwards corresponded with his landlord
there in Latin.

Next morning the ex-Anglican proselyte's first impulse was to pay his homage at the Tomb of the Apostles, when, as chance would have it, Pius IX. was in the act of realizing Scott's ballad—

> The Pope he was saying his High, High Mass
> All at St. Peter's shrine.

Their interview occurred in the crypt or subterranean sanctuary, the oldest portion of the basilica. It would appear that the inundations of Upper Italy opposed serious obstacles to the progress of the Oxford pilgrims, and that at one passage the cart which bore them, drawn by oxen, was well-nigh swallowed up by the rush of many waters. Safe from these semi-apostolic "perils of the flood," they are now engaged, under the guidance of the most intelligent of their countrymen and co-religionists, in a brief survey of whatever is most remarkable here ; and in a few days Mr. Newman, late of Oxford, and his companions will take possession of chambers in the College of Propaganda, and enter on a preparatory course previous to re-ordination in the Church of Rome.

Newman received Holy Orders at the hands of Cardinal Franzoni, and, in 1847, he announced, in a letter from Rome to Mr. Hope-Scott, the important plans already made—

We are to be Oratorians : Monsignor Brunelli went to the Pope about it the day before yesterday—my birthday. The Pope took up the plan most warmly. He wishes us to come here, as many as can, form a house under an experienced Oratorian Father, go through a novitiate, and return. I suppose we shall set up in Birmingham.

By the end of 1847 * he was back in London,

* Cardinal Manning, in his beautiful elegy on his brother Cardinal, speaks of having met him in Rome in 1848—a mistake of a year in the date.

which he reached on Christmas Eve. He went to Bishop Wiseman, who had now settled in Golden Square as Administrator of the London District; and all at once a great development of his plans was opened out. It happened in this wise. Frederick Faber, the Rector of Elton, who had called himself Newman's "acolyte" at Oxford, and who had been detained in Anglicanism by Newman's influential persuasions to patience, did not wait many days, once he heard of Newman's submission to the Church, to follow it by his own. Then he drifted to Birmingham, where Father Moore at St. Chad's had received many of the Oxford converts; and he had already formed himself and the friends who came with him from Elton into a sort of community in a Birmingham slum, when Newman first came to Maryvale. Faber's offer there and then to place himself and his companions under Newman, was declined; and before long Faber found himself and his fellows established at Cotton Hall, near Alton, by the Earl of Shrewsbury, who bought for him a piece of land to build upon beside the Catholic church at Cheadle. Here the "Brothers of the Will of God," or "Wilfridians," grew and prospered for eighteen months, until the time came, in Advent, 1847, when Faber should proceed to London to take the community vows

before Bishop Wiseman. Arriving in Golden
Square, he found, with Wiseman, Father Stanton,
just arrived from Rome—the first wearer of the
Oratorian habit in England. "Why not com-
bine?" said Wiseman—a thought which had
already taken possession of Father Faber. Why
not? The question was repeated to Father Newman, who arrived shortly afterwards, and to whom
Faber paid a visit at Maryvale, in January, 1848,
when all details were settled.

Next month Father Newman, with Stanton and
St. John, visited Faber at Cotton Hall, and formally
received Faber and his Wilfridians into the rule of
St. Philip Neri. Writing a few days afterwards,
Faber said: "Father Superior has now left us, all
in our Philippine habits, with turn-down collars,
like so many good boys brought in after dinner.
In the solemn admission, he gave us a most
wonderful address, full of those marvellous pauses.
He showed how, in his case and ours, St. Philip
seemed to have laid hands upon us, whether we
would or not. I hardly know what to do with
myself for very happiness." To Maryvale Faber
went, with Newman for his novice-master; but he
returned to Cotton Hall almost immediately; and
his novitiate ending, by dispensation, in July, 1848,
he became novice-master there to the new Com-

munity. In the month of October in that year, all the Fathers from Maryvale joined their brethren at Cotton Hall, at the instance of Bishop Wiseman. The Community were now forty in number, flourishing exceedingly. The ceremonies of the Church were carefully carried out, and Father Faber had already made some two hundred converts in the neighbourhood. Several lay friends came to live around; and Lord Arundel, Mr. David Lewis, Mrs. and Miss Bowden, may be called the nursing fathers and mothers of the infant congregation. Before this time a site in Bayswater had been offered to the Oratorians, by whom, however, it was declined, and it was afterwards to be the site of the Oblate Fathers' Church of St. Charles Borromeo and the home of Henry Edward Manning.

But no one had forgotten that for the town, and not for the country, was St. Philip's rule designed; and now Bishop Wiseman wrote to Father Newman asking him to come to London to found an Oratory there. Newman had already thought of Birmingham, and to the Pope had mentioned Birmingham as the place for his foundation. This, in Newman's opinion, was sufficient to allege as a reason for declining Bishop Wiseman's invitation. Great events have certainly been controlled everywhere by little incidents seemingly beneath the notice of

pompous records : the "Go it, Ned !" scrawled in
the corner of that despach of the Duke of Clarence's
which decided the Battle of Navarino, but is not
found in the Blue Books ; the chance wound which
led Ignatius of Loyola to take up the " Lives of
the Saints " as better than nothing in his boredom ;
the passing of Gibbon when Vespers were being
sung by monks by the Temple of Jupiter at
Rome ; the drowsiness of Ministers at a Richmond
dinner while the Duke of Newcastle read the letter
to Lord Raglan determining the invasion of the
Crimea; the badly cooked chop which lost Napoleon
Leipsic: all the innumerable littlenesses which
make up the domestic side of history. Newman's
ultimate settling at Birmingham has been assigned
to solemn causes : by some to his desire to hide
himself ; by others to the desire of his new
authorities that he should be hidden. Oh, what
a clatter of chatter if he had gone, as the Jesuit
proposed, to Timbuctoo ! We have heard enough
about the seclusion in Birmingham of this apostle
for whom, in truth, fine society had no fascinations,
of this man of letters who preserved in his seclusion
an almost uninterrupted literary mood. And, after
all, perhaps the determining reason was a substantial one—the weight of his books. These had
been carted to Maryvale at an incredible expense

—a sum equal to what had been half a year's income in his most flourishing Oxford days, when that yearly income, all told, never exceeded £500 a year. He had been moved already to Cotton Hall from Maryvale and from his books; not greatly liking the separation. They were a sort of magnet to him, and, as he could get to them more easily and less expensively than they to him —to them he went.

A house in Alcester Street, Birmingham, was taken, therefore, into which he entered in January, 1849. His first work was to draw up, with the help of those about him, lists of names of the Fathers who should stay at Birmingham, and of the Fathers who should be ceded to London. At last the approved list was sent to Cotton Hall to Faber, with a draft of the scheme for the foundation of the London Oratory, of which Faber was named the head. How it was formed, how it has flourished exceedingly, going from King William Street to South Kensington, needs not to be told here. Stanton and Dalgairns, late of Littlemore, were among those put on the London foundation; Bowles and St. John were among those who remained at Birmingham. Father Newman preached, on the opening day of the London Oratory, his sermon on the "Prospects of the Catholic Missioner." In 1850 he released the London Community from their obedience, and gave them "Home Rule," a system under which they have grown to be the centre of London's spiritual activity—far surpassing the parent Oratory in the glory of stone and marble, and in the size and splendour of appointments. Father Newman stayed at the Oratory in King William Street in 1852, for the Achilli trial; a time of excitement, during which he remained day and night, almost without interruption, before the Tabernacle.

The trial began in June, before Lord Campbell and a jury; and it lasted for several days. Giovanni Giacinto Achilli, an undoubted apostate priest, had lectured in Birmingham against Popery, representing himself as one who had escaped the persecutions of the Inquisition. What manner of man he really was, Newman set forth in one of the lectures on "The Position of Catholics." This was the crucial passage, the place of which is taken by stars only in subsequent editions of the "Lectures:"

The Protestant world flocks to hear him, because he has something to tell of the Catholic Church. He has something to tell, it is true ; he *has* a scandal to reveal, an argument to exhibit. That one argument is himself, it is his presence which is the triumph of Protestants ; it is the sight of him which is a Catholic's confusion. It is indeed a confusion that our Holy Mother could have had a priest like him. He feels the force of the argument, and he shows himself to the multitude that is gazing upon him. " Mothers of families," he seems to say, " gentle maidens, innocent children, look at me, for I am worth looking at. You do not see such a sight every day. Can any Church live over the imputation of such a production as I am? I have been a Roman priest and a hypocrite. I havè been a profligate under a cowl. I am that Father Achilli who, as early as 1826, was deprived of my faculty to lecture for an offence which my superiors did their best to conceal ; and who, in 1827, had already earned the reputation of a scandalous friar. I am that Achilli who, in the diocese of Viterbo, in February, 1831, robbed of her honour a young woman of eighteen ; who, in September, 1833, was found guilty of a second such crime in the case of a person of twenty-eight ; and who perpetrated a third in July, 1834, in the case of another, aged twenty-four. I am he who was afterwards found guilty of sins, similar or worse, in other towns of the neighbourhood. I am that son of St. Dominic who is known to have repeated the offence at Capua, in 1834 and 1835, and at Naples again in 1840, in the case of a child of fifteen. I am he who chose the sacristy of the church for one of these crimes, and Good Friday for another. I am that Cavaliere Achilli, who then went to Corfu, made the wife of a tailor faithless to her husband, and lived publicly with the wife of a chorus singer. I am that Professor in the Protestant College at Malta who, with two others, was dismissed from my post for offences which the authorities could not get themselves to describe. And now attend to me, such as I am, and you shall see what you shall see about the barbarity and profligacy of the inquisitors of Rome ! "

One of the apostate's reverend supporters insisted that he should bring an action, which was laid, in the first instance, against Messrs. Burns and Lambert, the publishers of the " Lectures ;" but the name of Dr. Newman, by leave of the Court, was substituted as that of the defendant. The defence (in the preparation of which Newman had the friendly help of Mr. Hope-Scott, Q.C.) consisted of twenty-three paragraphs of justification ; and woman after woman confronted the curious black-wigged man, who "smiled and smiled " as they denounced him as the perpetrator of their ruin. Against their evidence was pitted the denial of Achilli, and this prevailed. Newman was sentenced to pay a fine of £100, and to be imprisoned until it was paid. While the cheque was being written, a cordon of chairs was drawn around him, so that he might feel himself in custody; a detention which adds his name to the list of imprisoned law-breakers, with Shakspere and with Bunyan. The *Times*, speaking of the result of the trial, said : " To Protestants and Romanists, the case, truly viewed, is unimportant; its real significance is in the discredit it has tended to throw on our administration of justice, and the impression which it has tended to disseminate—that where religious differences come into play, a jury is the echo of popular feeling, instead of being the expositor of its own." *

---

* A quarter of a century later a point in the case was quoted in one of the Courts as a precedent, when the following dialogue took

The house in Alcester Street was poor enough
for a man who had lost in law expenses £10,000,
and the church adjoining was an old gin warehouse.
"British spirits, pass this way," was the legend
painted on an old iron door at the back of the
altar. To a recent writer in a Birmingham newspaper, who went to Alcester Street in those days,
and "saw John Henry Newman addressing a mere
handful—sometimes, perhaps, a couple of hundred
—of poor people, many of them Irish labourers," it
appeared that "Rome had lost the skill with which
she is credited of using with the greatest effective-
ness every instrument at her command. We happened to hear a discourse of his in those days in
which there was a brilliant sketch of Napoleon and
his influence on the national and religious life of
Europe. It was delivered on a week-night, and
the congregation, if we can trust to memory, did
not consist of more than forty people, most of
whom must have been very ill-educated." Newman
himself, not "Rome," judged differently, however ;
nor did he hesitate, when cholera broke out at
Walsall—doubtless also among "poor people" and

place :—Lord Chief Justice COCKBURN : The case referred to
created a painful impression on my mind, which can never be
effaced.—The SOLICITOR-GENERAL : Your Lordship was counsel in
it.—The LORD CHIEF JUSTICE : I was beaten, Mr. Solicitor ; and
I ought to have been the victor.

"mostly Irish"—to put his life at their disposal; taking, with Father St. John, the place of the priest already prostrated by his labours.

Meanwhile, the man of letters was not idle. The "Discourses to Mixed Congregations" were issued from this house. The lectures on "Difficulties felt by Anglicans" were here composed, in which, as also in the lectures on "The Present Position of Catholics in England," his style attained its high-water mark. These last-named lectures were delivered in the Birmingham Corn Exchange, the lecturer, who wore his habit, remaining seated, and reading from his MS. Admission was by ticket, and one ticket was held at the first lecture by "Mr. Manning, late Archdeacon." At the end of the course of nine lectures, Bishop Ullathorne thanked the lecturer, who made, in reply, a singular confession: "It is a curious thing for me to say that, though I am of mature age, and have been very busy in many ways, yet this is the first time in my life that I have ever received any praise." Beyond this hall the lectures were heard—and praised, too. George Eliot read them "with great amusement (!)"—the mark of exclamation her own —"they are full of clever satire and description."

# CHAPTER V.

## AT THE ORATORY, EDGBASTON.

The building of the Oratory—Mr. Spooner takes fright—
The daily life—An interval at Dublin—The Oratory
school—Newman as a talker—The literary work of the
period—The Cardinalate—"Home" after Rome—Rednal
—The last resting-place.

IN 1852 the Oratorians left Alcester Street for
Edgbaston, where they have since remained.
The plans for the house were drawn up by an
engineer, Mr. Terence Flannagan, a cousin of one
of the Fathers. During the building, some of the
Littlemore stories were again in the air ; and Father
Newman had to explain his kitchen arrangements
to the world in a letter to the *Times :*—

### UNDERGROUND CELLS.

May 15th, 1851.

SIR,

The *Times* newspaper has just been brought me,
and I see in it a report of Mr. Spooner's speech on the
Religious Houses Bill. A passage in it runs as follows : "It
was not usual for the coroner to hold an inquest, unless
when a rumour had got abroad that there was a necessity
for one ; and how was a rumour to come from the under-

ground cells of convents? Yes, he repeated, underground cells; and he would tell honourable members something about such places. At this moment, in the parish of Edgbaston, within the Borough of Birmingham, there was a large convent of some kind or other being erected, and the whole of the underground was fitted up with cells!" The house alluded to in this extract is the one I am building for the Congregation of the Oratory of St. Philip Neri, of which I am Superior. The underground cells to which Mr. Spooner refers have been devised in order to economize space for offices commonly attached to a large house. I think they are five in number, but I cannot be certain. They run under the kitchen and its neighbourhood. One is to be a larder, another is to be a coal-hole; beer, perhaps wine, may occupy a third. As to the rest, Mr. Spooner ought to know that we have had ideas of baking and brewing; but I cannot pledge myself to him that such will be their ultimate destination. Larger subterraneans commonly run under gentlemen's houses in London, but I have never in thought or word connected them with practices of cruelty and with inquests, and never asked their owners what use they made of them. When is this inquisition into the private matters of Catholics to end?

Your obedient servant,<br>
JOHN HENRY NEWMAN.

The church was merely four brick walls, requiring no design beyond that of the local builder. So it has since remained, with the addition of the sanctuary, planned by Mr. J. H. Pollen. The place has been described by a man who has at least the qualifications of being familiar with every corner of it. Writing about the year 1886, he says—

About a mile and a half from either of the Birmingham

F

railway stations a visitor who passes along the whole length of Broad Street to the " Five Ways," and then turns up the Hagley Road, in the pleasant suburb of Edgbaston, reaches a plain, substantial red-brick building on the right, which covers a very considerable piece of ground. It has no pretension to ecclesiastical style. The building adjoining, which has somewhat the appearance of a riding-school, and comes right up to the pavement with an almost unbroken red-brick frontage of some eighty feet, is the big room of the Oratory School in which the well-known Latin plays are annually performed ; and an ostentatiously plain door at the nearer end of it, open in the morning and evening, leads to the Oratory Church, through a pleasing little round-arched cloister, which bears marks rather of ingenious contrivance than of any boldly conceived design. The church itself will probably disappoint the visitor, as it is small and dingy and without any architectural feature of interest, being, in fact, only a temporary building that has undergone alteration from time to time. The careful observer may, however, find in odd corners a bit of mosaic or of marble work that will please him ; but where imitative decorations mainly prevail, the lover of the genuine is apt to distrust everything. The plain oaken pulpit is that occupied at irregular intervals by Dr. Newman until two or three years ago ; and up a passage behind a statue of St. Joseph will be found the small and dark chapel of " Bona Mors," where he daily said Mass at seven in the morning, until his elevation to the Sacred College gave him the privilege of doing so in his own private room. On the spectator's left of the high altar is the Cardinal's throne, where, unless indisposed, he presides at the chief ceremony on the great festivals of the Church, and notably at the High Mass on the Feast of St. Philip Neri (May 26th) and on that of the Immaculate Conception December 8th).

The cost of the Achilli case may, perhaps, partly account for the poverty and inadequacy of the

Oratory Church at Birmingham. It had been in the Cardinal's thoughts to build a worthier, one which would in miniature recall St. Mark's at Venice, the church he most of all admired; and M. Viollet le Duc came to Birmingham and prepared plans. But the "libel" trial timed with the entrance of the Fathers into the new house at Edgbaston; and Newman used to say that he had not the heart to ask for aid to build a big church after the inflowing of subscriptions to defray his legal expenses. Heavy as these were, there was a surplus of money subscribed; to be re-spent partly in Ireland, which had given, as usual, abundantly out of its own poverty.

There, at Edgbaston, for thirty-eight years, he lived, laboured, and loved. The little break made, early in the time, by his residence in Dublin as Rector of the Irish Catholic University, hardly destroys the continuity of that long spell of peaceful years. He was still "the Father" in his experimental absence; an experiment which did not succeed. Nor did he in Ireland cut himself off from old friends. The men of the Oxford Movement were gathered about him, his own converts, some of them: Mr. Allies, who has told the story of his momentous "Life's Decision;" Mr. Aubrey de Vere, the link between the vitalizing of poetry by

Wordsworth and Tennyson—his friends—and the vitalizing of religion by Newman and Manning—himself a sharer alike in the literary and in the religious glory ; Henry Bedford, who once well compared plain Father Newman to Napoleon, wearing no star among his generals who wore—constellations ; J. H. Pollen, formerly a clergyman, and afterwards to fill more than one responsible post in the world of art and of politics ; Le Page Renouf, the first of scholars in phases of Biblical history—now of the British Museum ; Thomas Arnold, the son of Dr. Arnold and the brother of Matthew ; Robert Ornsby, the biographer of Hope-Scott ; Penny, who had been a visitor at Littlemore after his resignation of his living and his reception, before Newman's, into the Church ; and W. H. Anderdon, who afterwards as a Jesuit Father fulfilled his apostolate, or continues it from Heaven. The lectures on " University Education " were delivered in Dublin ; and the fame and name of Newman still inhabit the city from which he retired, at the end of 1859, with the conviction that he had served " a country which had tokens in her of an important future, and the promise of still greater works than she has yet achieved in the cause of the Catholic faith."

Dublin or Oxford dwelt, for a time, in Newman's

thoughts, as alternative places for an attempt to establish a College of high aims for Catholics. Dublin fell through, and the Oxford attempt was never made ; for it failed, for good or for ill, to win the final approval of Pius IX., though Cardinals and others, including many fathers of sons, awaited its accomplishment with hopes and blessings. The Oratory School, established at Birmingham in 1859, supplied a smaller need, but supplied it well. One " Old Boy," Mr. Arthur Pollen, recalls :—

At the Oratory we saw a good deal of the Cardinal ; and, although he took no active share in the administration of the school, his interest in it was always great. Nothing pleased him more than making friends with the boys, and the many opportunities we had of personal contact with him made the friendship a real one. Of course, to us he was the greatest of heroes. Slight and bent with age, with head thrust forward, and a quick firm gait, the great Oratorian might often be seen going from corridor to corridor, or across the school grounds. His head was large, the pink biretta made it seem still more so, and he carried it as if the neck were not strong enough for the weight. His face changed but little ; yet he would be a bold man who attempted to describe its sweetness, its firmness, and its strength. A pontifical ring and red sash and biretta were the only symbols of his rank ; and no one living in the Oratory would imagine that it was the home of a Prince of the Holy Roman Church. It had been his special desire from the beginning that no ceremony or state should be maintained. He was always known by those in the house as " the Father ; " and except in the part he took in the ceremonies of the Church, his dignity made small difference to his life. In the Latin plays which he had prepared for the boys to act he always took the keenest interest, insisting on the careful rendering of favourite passages, and himself giving hints in cases of histrionic difficulty. In the school chapel he from time to time appeared, giving a short address, and assisting at the afternoon service. It is curious that it should have been in connection with these two widely different occupations that we should have seen most of him. It is, perhaps, characteristic of his disposition, in which playfulness and piety were so sweetly combined.

Another "Old Boy," Dr. Sparrow, also remembers some of the methods and moods of his master :—

The first boy to arrive was the eldest son of Serjeant Bellasis—R. G. Bellasis, who afterwards joined the Congregation of the Oratory, and is now Father Richard Bellasis, of the Birmingham Oratory. I went myself to the Oratory in 1863, and for eleven years enjoyed the privilege and blessing of the Cardinal's training. In those early days of the school we saw more of the Father (as we called him) than was possible for the students to have done in later years, owing to his age and physical weakness. Every month, in my time, each form went up to the Father's room and was examined by him *vivâ voce* in the work done during the preceding month, a trying ordeal for those who were nervous or idle, notwithstanding the kindness and gentleness of the Father, who was one of the most considerate and sympathetic of examiners. The Father always attached great importance to the "lesson by heart," and insisted on perfect accuracy and readiness in its repetition. He was always most particular to urge upon the boys a higher standard of honour, and never would tolerate anything mean or shabby. At the end of each term every boy went to the Father for what we called his "character," that is, the Father spoke to him privately as to his progress and behaviour during the past term. There was a story that in the early days of the school the Father received about the same time a letter from A., who had a boy at the school, complaining that the vacation was too long, and a letter from B., who also had a son at the school, complaining that the vacation was too short ; Dr. Newman quietly (after cutting off the signatures) sent A.'s letter to B., and B.'s letter to A., after which no more was heard from either on the subject.   When I was reading for the London University Intermediate Examinations in Arts along with another, the Father took us himself in classics and English literature, and I shall never forget those lectures, especially those in literature.   He told us how greatly he admired Sir Walter Scott's novels ; he also expressed a great liking for the " Rejected Addresses," as some of the cleverest parodies he had read ; and he encouraged us to read good novels.

The life of the Fathers of the Oratory differs little from that of any group of secular priests living in community.   A visitor to Edgbaston in the early 'eighties, Mr. C. Kegan Paul, gives the following account of the domestic routine :—

Each Father has his own comfortable room,* library and bedroom in one, the bed within a screen, the crucifix above, and the prized personal little fittings on the walls.   The library is full of valuable books, many of them once the private property of Dr. Newman, now forming the nucleus of a stately collection for the use of the Community.   The quiet men who share this home come and go about their several businesses—the care of the school, whose buildings join, but are separate from the Oratory proper, the work in the church, in hearing confessions, saying Masses, and preaching.   In the house the long soutane and biretta are worn ; to go abroad they wear the usual dress of the clergy

---

* " The Father," however, had two rooms allotted to him.

in England.   Perhaps it is the dinner-hour, and the silent
figures pass along the galleries to the refectory, a lofty room
with many small tables, and a pulpit at one end opposite the
tables.   At one of these sits the Superior alone, clad like
the rest save the red lines of his biretta, which mark his
Cardinal's rank.   But among his children, and in his home,
he is still more the Superior and the Father than a Prince
of the Church.   At a table near him may, perhaps, be a
guest, and at others the members of the Community, two
and two.   The meal is served by two of the Fathers, who
take this office in turn ; and it is only of late that Dr.
Newman has himself ceased to take his part in this brotherly
service, owing to his advanced years.   During the meal a
novice reads from the pulpit a chapter of the Bible, then
a short passage from the life of St. Philip Neri, and then
from some book, religious or secular, of general interest.
The silence is otherwise unbroken save for the words needful
in serving the meal.   Towards the end, one of the Fathers
proposes two questions for discussion, or rather for utterance
of opinion.   On one day there was a point of Biblical criticism
proposed, and one of ecclesiastical etiquette (if the word
may be allowed) ; whether, if a priest, called in haste to
administer Extreme Unction, did so inadvertently with the
sacred oil set apart for another purpose, instead of that for
Unction, the act was gravely irregular.   Each gave his
opinion on one or other of these questions, the Cardinal on
the first, gravely, and in well-chosen words.   Yet it seemed
to the observer that, while he, no doubt, recognized that such
a point must be decided and might have its importance,
there was a certain impatience in the manner in which he
passed by the ritual question and fastened on that proposed
from Scripture.   After this short religious exercise, the com-
pany passed into another room for a frugal dessert and glass
of wine, since the day chanced to be a feast ; and there was
much to remind an Oxford man of an Oxford Common-
room, the excellent talk sometimes to be heard there, and
the dignified unbending for a while from serious thought.

As a talker in the old days Newman has been described by Mr. J. A. Froude :—

Newman's mind was world-wide. He was interested in everything which was going on in science, in politics, in literature. Nothing was too large for him, nothing too trivial, if it threw light upon the central question, what man really was, and what was his destiny. His natural temperament was bright and light ; his senses, even the commonest, were exceptionally delicate. He could admire enthusiastically any greatness of action and character, however remote the sphere of it from his own. Gurwood's " Despatches of the Duke of Wellington" came out just then. Newman had been reading the book, and a friend asked him what he thought of it. " Think?" he said ; " it makes one burn to have been a soldier ! " He seemed always to be better informed on common topics of conversation than any one else who was present. He was never condescending with us (undergraduates), never didactic or authoritative ; but what he said carried conviction along with it. Perhaps his supreme merit as a talker was that he never tried to be witty or to say striking things. Ironical he could be, but not ill-natured. Not a malicious anecdote was ever heard from him. Prosy he could not be. He was lightness itself—the lightness of elastic strength—and he was interesting because he never talked for talking's sake, but because he had something real to say.

At Littlemore he had told his young men to drop the *Mister.* " Call me Newman," he said. But on this point they were not bold enough to obey. " The Vicar " was a good way out of the difficulty then, as " The Father " was at the Oratory, where he called the others by their Christian names— " William " and " John ;" proving that a title is

not always the useless "tin-kettle" which Lord
Strangford found his own. Archdeacon George
Anthony Denison speaks of the Oriel Common-
room in 1828, attended by "Whately, Arnold,
Blanco White, Keble, Newman, Hampden," and
others, as being "as dull a place socially as I can
remember anywhere"—"there was no freedom of
intercourse." But Mozley, also a Fellow, supposes
the Archdeacon must have forgotten all about
Oriel, since he jumbles together names of men he
can never have seen together there. Probably,
Newman and his intimates did not unbosom themselves to Denison; possibly, Newman received
some of his statements with even that withering
"Really!" after hearing which you were supposed
to go and hide yourself. Certain it is that Newman
told him in later years that "he was sorry for
instances of harshness" towards him during their
time at Oriel. Denison answered that he had no
recollection of any such instances, but, if such
there were, it must have been that Newman was
far more in earnest than he.

Newman, then and afterwards, was never wanting
in tact as a talker. Father Bertrand Wilberforce,
O.P., writes to me: "A characteristic story used to
be told by my dearest father.* When Newman

---

* Henry Wilberforce, who resigned the living of East Farleigh

was Fellow of Oriel, during the Hampden controversy, an American professor visited Oxford and
dined at the high table. As the Fellows took
different views in the controversy, it was never
mentioned at dinner. . The American, not understanding this, suddenly cried out: 'Well, Mr.
Newman, what about this Hampden controversy?'
Newman at once seized a spoon, and taking a
potato from the dish, said: 'A hot potato?'"
Another time, when a naval chaplain was em-
barrassed by being asked whether his service on
board ship was "High" or "Low," Newman inter-
posed : "Surely that depends upon the tide." His
own peculiar method of turning off questions which
were not timely is well known. "Serious compli-
cations in Rome, Father," said Lord Edward
Howard,* a member of Parliament anxious to get
at Newman's mind during a crisis of the Roman
question. "Yes," said the Father, quickly adding :
"And in China." And there was something in

to become a Catholic, and to whom Newman dedicated "Callista" :
"To you alone, who have known me so long, and who love me so
well, could I venture to offer a trifle such as this. But you will
recognize the author in his work and take pleasure in the recognition." It is Henry Wilberforce who forms the most charming and
human figure in all the group of Newman's contemporaries sketched
by Mr. Mozley.

* Afterwards first Lord Howard of Glossop, whom Newman
came to London purposely to see upon his death-bed.

his manner, we suppose, which prevented his ques-
tioners on such occasions from feeling that they
were being trifled with. When he knew words
would be wasted, he would not spend them. One
of those about him having resolved to leave him,
under circumstances likely to raise exclamations
and to invite remonstrance, told him his determination. " By what train ? " was all he said in
acceptance of the inevitable. His offer to the
Protestant champion who challenged him to a
discussion, that he would play him on the violin,
was another instance of his economy of words.

Many were the visitors from afar who sought out
the Father at the Oratory : strangers and wayfarers,
generally in anxiety about their souls ; old friends,
too, some of whom, like Lord Emly and Aubrey
de Vere, made a point of paying him a yearly visit.
There, when both were bowed with age, met the
two great Cardinals—the friends, counterparts and
contrasts during sixty years. In the 'eighties they
had half an hour together in Birmingham : saying
not much, but looking each at each, with what self-
revelations, what leave-takings ! When the news of
death came from Birmingham, the Prince of the
Church at Westminster — though eight years
younger—bowed his head and said he felt he had
his own notice to quit. Some went to the Oratory,

as it were by night. Other business brought them
to the Midlands: politics, for example. The last
time Mr. Gladstone visited the house thc invalid
could not see him ; but the politician, hearing that
the Cardinal's arrangements for reading when
reclining were defective, supplied a remedy. And
there were some who were not even as Nicodemus ;
who were drawn to the Oratory, but never went.
" I envy you your opportunity of seeing and
hearing Newman," wrote George Eliot to Miss
Hennell ; "and I should like to make an expedi-
tion to Birmingham with that sole end." If only
she had gone !

It was the " Apologia," written at Edgbaston in
1864, that did much more than confute Kingsley—
it "breathed new life into me," said George Eliot,
who, so speaking, spoke too for others. " Pray
mark," she writes, "that beautiful passage in which
he thanks his friend, Ambrose St. John. I know
hardly anything that delights me more than such
evidence of sweet brotherly love being a reality in
the world." In 1866 Newman wrote at Birmingham his answer to Pusey's " Eirenicon : " " There
was one of old time who wreathed his sword in
myrtle; excuse me, you discharge your olive-branch
as if from a catapult." In 1870 the " Grammar
of Assent " was published ; and five years later he

issued his " Letter to the Duke of Norfolk on Mr.
Gladstone's Expostulations:" taking this very
welcome opportunity for linking his name with that
of one of the Old Boys of the Oratory School who
was dear to him. Perhaps the life of the man of
letters at Edgbaston was a more even one than it
had ever been elsewhere : bringing with it no great
discoveries, or fears, or surprises. He did not again
"see a ghost:"— such as he had encountered in 1839,
when the history of the fifth century revealed to
him that the old Monophysite heresy was a type
of Anglicanism ; and such as reappeared to him in
1842 while translating Athanasius. He did not
laugh to himself any longer as he had laughed at
Maryvale over his composition of " Loss and Gain "
—with its peculiar convert-clerical irony. He did
not feel again the thrill of pleasure which ran
through him as he took down the volumes of the
Fathers from the shelves at Littlemore, after he
had been received into the Church, and said, " You
are mine now, you are mine now : " this nearest
approach to almost bridal joy and sense of possession and triumph at last after long wooing, experienced by the lonely student, who had felt
himself called to lead a single life from his youth,
and for whom pleasure held out no temptations.

In truth, the most disturbing event of the

Edgbaston period was the publication in the *Standard* of the private letter he had written— with a pen primed with panic, the pen of a recluse —during the sittings of the Vatican Council, to Bishop Ullathorne—between whom and himself the relations were always affectionate. And it "took away his breath" to find, one morning in 1885, among his letters one from Frank Power's sister, to say that she possessed a relic from Khartoum—a copy of "The Dream of Gerontius," given to her brother by Gordon, and scored by Gordon with incisive pencil-marks at such passages as, "Now that the hour is come, my fear is fled," and "Pray for me, O my friends." This poem, in which penetrating sincerity of feeling on a great subject finds the most poetical expression attained by Newman, was sent by him, in the first instance, to a periodical, the editor of which asked him for something: "I have routed this out of a drawer."

From Birmingham he had now and again to make a profession of Faith:—

I have not had one moment's wavering of trust in the Catholic Church ever since I was received into her fold. I hold, and ever have held, a supreme satisfaction in her worship, discipline, and teaching ; and an eager longing, and a hope against hope, that the many dear friends whom I have left in Protestantism may be partakers in my happiness. And I do hereby profess that Protestantism is the dreariest of possible religions ; that the thought of the Anglican service makes me shiver, and the thought of the Thirty-nine Articles makes me shudder. Return to the Church of England ! No ! " The net is broken, and we are delivered." I should be a consummate fool (to use a mild term) if, in my old age, I left " he land flowing with milk and honey " for the city of confusion and the house of bondage.

He was only sixty-one, and had still a third of his life to run when he was writing thus of his " old age." The first letter I ever had from him, written early in 1874, ends: " Don't forget in your prayers that I am very old now, and need every help I can get from friends." For twenty years there were such closing passages and post-scripts to letters addressed alike to friend and casual correspondent, postscripts always pene-trating. By 1887 it had got to " Excuse a short letter—but I do not write without pain ;" and the signature became as much as he could easily attempt at the end of the text indited in a hand rather freer than his own, but closely formed upon it, by his faithful friend and devoted other-self, Father William Neville.*

The news of his impending elevation to the

* One of the six Anglican clergymen connected with St. Saviour's, Leeds, received into the Church together by Father Newman in 1851.

Cardinalate reached Newman at the Oratory early in 1879 by rumour; and in March a letter from Cardinal Manning, giving an all but official message to that effect from the Pope, put an end to the "suspense" he said he felt while the news seemed to be known to everybody, but to him had never been formally announced. His was not the attitude of St. Bonaventura, who looked up from washing dishes in the kitchen to tell the Pope's messengers to hang up the hat in the passage. It was no bauble to Newman, whose respect for authority was the mainspring of his Anglican as of his Catholic life, and gave a value, in his eyes, to a recognition from the Father of Christendom. It was a seal set upon his fidelity by Leo XIII., who was wont to refer to him affectionately as "my Cardinal." It closed controversies which, while they lasted, had been sometimes hot, and always disturbing; vexed questions about an Oratorian establishment at Oxford; about the opportuneness of the Vatican Council's definition; about the dogmatism of Dr. Ward and the *Dublin Review;* about his general, but strictly conditioned, sympathy with the writers in the suppressed *Rambler.* It was a pledge of good will from a quarter which, by rewarding him so highly, practically imposed silence on the old opponents. "They are all on my side now," said

G

the aged Cardinal with a smile : a smile which had no poor human triumphing in it, but an added indulgent sweetness. Pusey did not quite understand how much it meant, when he wrote to Newman to congratulate him on his having the offer of the Cardinalate, and on his alleged refusal of it. Writing later, Pusey said : " His still life in the Oratory at Birmingham had been an ideal to me. However, dear Newman thought that it would have been ungrateful in him towards those who had been at the pains to obtain this honour for him, and he accepted it, though he himself preferred obscurity. . . . Nothing has or can come between my deep love for John Henry Newman." In truth the old "still life in the Oratory" was not broken, when once the new Cardinal had been in Rome and received his hat—choosing *Cor ad cor loquitur* as his motto, and St. George in Velabro as his titular church. It was the same still life, and the old retiring John Henry Newman ; but it was the life crowned with the only glory he sought, the approbation of the living Church : a glory which, like the " harrowing praise " in Coventry Patmore's " Odes," humbles even while it exalts.*

* Dr. Döllinger, who, during his last years, gave up to gossip a mind meant for history, said Newman's elevation showed that

Back to Birmingham he came, after weariness in Rome, in July, 1879. "To come home again!" he said to the flock who gathered to meet him— "in that word 'home' how much is included! I know well that there is a more heroic life than a home-life. We know St. Paul's touching words in which he says he is an outcast. We know, too, that our Blessed Lord had not where to lay His head. But the idea of home is consecrated to us by St. Philip, who made it the very essence of his religious institute. Therefore I do indeed feel pleasure in coming home again." A few visits of a few days' duration through the ten remaining and declining years were the only absences from Edgbaston, except the stays at Rednal—the country-house of the Oratorians.

The end came at last quickly. There had been little illnesses ; and the failure of strength was so apparent that it seemed as if a breath or a movement would extinguish the faint spark. On one of

"his real views are not known at Rome," cheaply adding that "several of his works, had he written in French, Italian, or Latin, would have found a place on the 'Index.'" This opinion was printed and shown to Newman, who wrote : "It has pained me very much as manifesting a soreness and want of kindness for me which I did not at all suppose he felt. It makes one smile to suppose that Romans, of all men in the world, are wanting in acuteness, or that there are not quite enough men in the world who would be ready to convict me of heterodoxy if they could."

these days he asked some of the Fathers to come in and play or sing to him Father Faber's hymn of " The Eternal Years." When they had done so once, he made them repeat it, and this several times. "Many people," he said, "speak well of my 'Lead, kindly Light,' but this is far more beautiful. Mine is of a soul in darkness—this of the eternal light." Into that light he wakened up on Monday evening, the 11th of August, 1890, in the ninetieth year of his age.

It was impossible on the day of the funeral—a day also of fruition—not to think of that other day at Littlemore, when he entered the fold on earth which is one with the fold in heaven. Above and between the solemn chants, I was haunted by the words which " A Young Convert " has said, and which older converts say in measure, on the day of reception into the Church—

> " Who knows what days I answer for to-day ?
> Giving the bud, I give the flower.  I bow
> This yet unfaded and a faded brow.
> Bending these knees, and feeble knees, I pray.
> Thoughts yet unripe in me I turn one way ;
> Give one repose to pain I know not now ;
> One leaven to joy that comes I guess not how.
> I dedicate my fields when spring is grey.

> " O rash (I smile) to pledge my hidden wheat !
> I fold to-day, at altars far apart,
> Hands trembling with what toils !  In their retreat

I sign my love to come, my folded art.
I light the tapers at my head and feet,
And lay the crucifix on this silent heart."

Well had John Henry Newman's forty-five years
of Catholic life answered to the great act of the
ninth of October, 1845. To the Catholic Church
indeed he came, not in the bud, but in full flower of
his maturity. At its altars how faithfully knelt the
knees, at first firm, but afterwards feeble with the
weight of ninety years! Nor was he once disappointed, during all these forty-five years, of the
" repose " he had invoked at Littlemore for coming
pain. At "altars far apart "—in London, in Rome,
in Dublin, above all, at Birmingham—he had folded
" hands trembling with what toils ; " and in that
safe shelter he had been surrounded by his dearest
friends, and had practised the art of the penman
in full perfection. And now, at last, were lighted
those tapers at his head and feet ; and now was
that crucifix laid upon his silent heart. The forty-
five years since he first faced that final scene
seemed now but a moment in the wonderful dream.
The seal had been set on that October day for
ever and ever, and no man could break it. By
that day, all eternity was tinged.

At Rednal he was laid to rest by loving hands.
His grave he shares with Ambrose St. John, who

died in 1875, and in whose memory Newman
planted the now spreading bed of St. John's wort
down one side of the small enclosure. They loved
each other in life ; in death they are not divided.
On either side is a grave—that of Father Edward
Caswall, and that of Father J. Gordon. Two other
graves are there : that of Robert Boland, who died
while a novice ; and that of a son of Father Pope
—an Oratorian after the death of his wife. Thus
do tender human relationships cling—as is fitting
in presence of the ashes of that human heart—
to the graveyard where Cardinal Newman lies.

Even the dust of a woman is in that last resting-
place of celibacy : Frances Wootten, widow of the
Oxford doctor who attended the inmates of the
monastery at Littlemore ; she who had followed
Newman, first into the Church, and then . to
Birmingham to be the Matron, the Vice-Mother,
at the Oratory School. And my last words shall
leave him in association with women. He, who
gave himself to none, belonged to all ; becoming
the tender father and helper to many of that sex
which intimately enters into the life of a St. Paul
by Damaris, of a St. Francis de Sales by Madame
de Chantal. Among the flowers sent to Rednal,
were two wreaths, one of which bore the name of
a woman who offered it "to the most dear memory

of Cardinal Newman, who has been benefactor, guide, and counsellor through life." Another garland came from the Baroness Burdett-Coutts, as "a tribute of respect to a great Englishman, whose beauty of life shed its light of purity over his own century, but belongs to all ages:" a legacy that shall endure, by time untarnished and undimmed by death.

## CHAPTER VI.

### THE OUTER WORLD.

A MAN is entered in a Biographical Dictionary by the date of his birth ; but it is really the date of death that ranges him in the memories of mankind. Macaulay and Newman belong to a different epoch, but were born within a month or two of each other. Newman was a baby when Keats, a child of four or five, had not yet even heard of Lemprière. Shelley, just over eight, was already exciting the admiration of his sisters by his declamation of Latin verse. Byron was beginning his tumultuous teens, scribbling his first verses, and being well hated at Harrow. Newman hardly ranks as the contemporary of these, though he was twenty when Keats died, was of age when Shelley died, and when Byron died was twenty-three. With Coleridge, Southey, and Wordsworth, though these were all born between thirty and thirty-five years before him, he lived for thirty-three, forty-two, and forty-nine years. In 1836,

Faber, returning to Oxford from the Long, which
he had spent at the Lakes, reported that " Wordsworth spoke of Newman's sermons, some of which
he had read and liked exceedingly." Walter Scott
was thirty when Newman was born, and when
Scott died Newman was beginning the Tractarian
movement which was to give Abbotsford to
Rome.

Newman's literary admirations were in great
part those of the period. For Scott he had all
Mr. Gladstone's enthusiasm. The tinsel of that
mediævalism did not disconcert him ; and he grate-
fully mentions Scott as having in some sort, by
his scenes of chivalry, prepared the path for the
Catholic revival ; surely a route to the Oratory
by way of Wardour Street! Scott's novels he put
into the hands of the boys at the Oratory school
at Edgbaston as prizes, and even examined in
them. Perhaps he had his happiest holiday when
he spent five weeks at Abbotsford at the end of
1852, the guest of Mr. Hope-Scott, who, like his
wife, Lockhart's daughter, had become a Catholic.
When Newman got the invitation he wrote in
reply : " It would be a great pleasure to spend
some time with you, and then I have ever had
the extremest sympathy for Walter Scott, and it
would delight me to see his place. When he was

dying, I was saying prayers (whatever they were worth) for him continually, thinking of Keble's words, 'Think on the minstrel as ye kneel.'" Lockhart was still alive, and the visits his daughter and son-in-law paid him in London, he repaid at Abbotsford, whither, finally, he had his books taken. There, in the breakfast-room, because he could not leave the ground-floor, and because he shunned the dining-room where Sir Walter gave up the ghost, the old editor, a stoic amid suffering, a Protestant among Catholics, passed away, with Father Lockhart, a distant cousin, at his unresponsive side, and the sound of his daughter's voice, reading prayers from her "Garden of the Soul," in his ears.

One can well imagine the mystification of the old editor of the *Quarterly* in presence of the Popery which sat at his hearth, although he had been willing to give Tractarianism a distant hearing in his Review. In 1837, one of the party at Oxford complacently records that "Lockhart finds he must have an infusion of Oxford principles; it takes with people now—that is, such people as read the *Quarterly;*" and Philip Pusey, the member of Parliament, told his brother Edward that one of Newman's greatest triumphs was his "getting hold of the *Quarterly.*" A little later this com-

placency must have been shaken by the report
that Murray had said he would have given a
thousand pounds to be able to suppress the article
which Sewell had written.

Though the *Quarterly* might turn half an ear
timidly towards the arresting preacher of St. Mary
the Virgin, such leniency could not be expected
from the rival Review. Of course Macaulay was
cock-sure, even *before* reading one of Newman's
Anglican books, that he could reply to it. Writing
to the editor of the *Edinburgh*, Napier, in February,
1843, he says : " I hear much of a defence of the
miracles of the third and fourth centuries by
Newman. I have not yet read it. I think that I
could treat that subject without giving any scandal
to any rational person ; and I should like it much.
The times require a Middleton." There was no
weak openness to conviction lurking behind those
words ; nor yet behind these, written eight months
later, also to Napier, and also before he had read the
book he was eager to smash : " Newman announces
an English hagiology in numbers which is to
contain the lives of such blessed saints as Thomas
à Becket and Dunstan. I should not dislike to be
the devil's advocate on such an occasion." In his
essay on the " Comic Dramatists of the Restora-
tion," Macaulay just alludes to the Tractarians,

saying that Jeremy Collier's notions touching "the importance of vestments, ceremonies, and solemn days, differed little from those which are now held by Dr. Pusey and Mr. Newman"—a sentence which suggests to the initiated that the writer wrote once more without having read Newman— who was never a Ritualist, and treasured no husk except it held a kernel.

After all, it was left to Sir James Stephen and to Henry Rogers to pillory Popery in the pages of the *Edinburgh.* The first of these, after confessing in a letter to Napier, in 1841, that whatever comes he "cannot but cherish the good old Protestant feelings of our ancestors," thus conveniently explains away Mr. Newman : "As for Newman himself, I am sorry that his integrity should be impugned. I am convinced that a more upright man does not exist. But his understanding is essentially illogical and inveterately imaginative ; and I have reason to fear that he labours under a degree of cerebral excitement, which unfits him for the mastery of his own thoughts and the guidance of his own pen." It is worth noting, that while Newman was being thus described on hearsay as a literary lunatic, Pusey, his constant companion, was writing of him to a friend : "You will be glad to hear that the immediate excitement about

Tract 90 is subsiding. It has been a harassing time for N., but he was wonderfully calm."

Macaulay, instead of reading the books he had already prejudged, probably contented himself with reading the *Edinburgh* attack on them (April, 1843), and not all of that. "I have read three or four pages of the article on the Puseyites, which I like very much. I should be glad to know who wrote it." The writer was Henry Rogers, who congratulated himself with the true Whig confidence, when he sent his MS. to the editor, that he had "not spared ridicule" in treating "publications which are having a large sale, and are doing immense mischief amongst the young, the ardent, and the sentimental." But "the young, the ardent, and the sentimental" had grown into men and reviewers by the time the "Apologia" appeared ; and Newman, for the first time, found himself seriously considered, whether favourably or not, by secular publications.

Indeed, "the young, the ardent, and the sentimental" of the early 'forties had made themselves felt in the other walks of life, as well as in literature, before many years were over. They manned the Anglican Church. Rival Cabinet Ministers might be seen sitting under the same Tractarian shepherd in Mayfair. A Lord Chief

Justice ranked it as his highest honour to be the
host of Cardinal Newman, even after his secession;
and there was no house in London where he was
more welcome than at the Deanery of St. Paul's.
Dean Church was one of that immense body of
actual contemporaries or immediate juniors who
came under Newman's personal influence, and who,
in their turn, spread the principles which have
transformed the Anglican .Communion.  In one
sense the *Guardian* expresses the bare truth when
it speaks of Newman as "the founder of the
Anglican Church as it now is," and says : "Great
as his services have been to the Communion in
which he died, they are as nothing by the side
of those he rendered to the Communion in which
the most eventful years of his life were spent.
He will be mourned by many in the Roman
Church ; but their sorrow will be less than ours,
because they have not the same paramount reason
to be grateful to him."  Not in admiration for his
mind, nor in reverence for his character, nor in
personal devotion yielded him even by strangers,
can those to whom he came be outstripped by
those whom he left.  His life was divided with a
strange equality of time between the two Communions ; for he lived in each for half of it almost
to a month.  But he actually changed the face

of the Anglican Church, while he could not alter one feature of the immutable other.

Of all his contemporaries, therefore, the Anglican clergy bear most the marks of him. What their predecessors were seventy years ago, when Newman began " to come out of his shell," has ceased to be a memory, but it remains as a tradition. " Decent, easy men, who supremely enjoyed the gifts of the founder, from the toil of reading, thinking, or writing they had absolved their conscience. Their conversation stagnated in a round of college business, Tory politics, personal anecdotes, and private scandal. Their dull and deep potations excused the intemperance of youth." Such were the Oxford dons of an earlier generation, as described by Gibbon, Newman's greatest master in style, and his finger-post to the Fathers. " Whenever you meet a clergyman of my time," said Sydney Smith to Mr. Gladstone about the year 1835, "you may be sure he is a bad clergyman ; " and Sydney Smith had as little love as Gibbon himself would have had for " Puseyism."

Vainly was Evangelicalism pitched against "two-bottle orthodoxy." In Wesley, Newman as a Catholic recognized "the shadow of a Catholic saint ; " but the name of Wesley worked no wonders in the Oxford of Newman's early days.

The Evangelicals entrenched themselves in an obscure college, and their influence never spread beyond St. Edmund's Hall. Mozley says it may have been a common peculiarity of their complexions, but the St. Edmund's men never looked clean. He adds that their mental and moral claims to influence were inconspicuous; and Archbishop Tait of Canterbury admits that there is too much truth in this ugly delineation. Newman and his friends, on the other hand, joined learning with sanctity, and united good-breeding with unworldliness. "We loved the Evangelicals because they loved our Lord," said Pusey—a formula which sums up the Catholic attitude towards the Salvation Army to-day; but that is the beginning and the end of the bond; and Newman saw, even if Keble did not, that liberalism in religion, represented by Whately and the rest, was a force Evangelicalism could not touch: that Evangelicalism was itself only another form of liberalism, though the feelings and prejudices of its adherents were on the side of personal religiousness. The men who had a general idea of the importance of dogma, but who had not the enthusiasm of religion, and the men who had the enthusiasm but no science or coherence, met together under Newman, and supplied to each other the deficiency of each.

The leaders themselves—Newman, Pusey, and Keble—united tender personal piety with a zeal for dogmatic exactitude—for truth in thought as well as in conduct.

The reasons why the early leadership seemed to lie with Pusey, and not with Newman, are well known. Equally well known is it that Newman was the mainspring of the movement. " Out of my own head," he says he started the Tracts, and the Tracts became the text-books of the new Anglicanism. The doctrines they expounded, though fresh to the hearers, were old as the Apostles, and were gathered by Newman from the Bible he loved and studied ; they had been taught without intermission by the Catholic Church from the first Peter to the last Leo ; and the Anglican Church itself, under Archbishop Laud, fitfully received them. The result of Newman's labour as a revivalist is seen to-day in half the rectories of England. The typical Anglican minister trains, conducts, even dresses himself on the model of the Catholic priest ; and if externals could make him the real thing, the real thing he would perfectly be. Beautiful were the tributes which Newman's death elicited from the conspicuous pulpits of Anglicanism, and most affecting to Catholics ; but surely some of the preachers strangely misunderstood their master

H

when they hinted that he might never have left
Anglicanism in 1845 had he foreseen how many
Roman collars would be worn, how many beards
be shaved off, how many "celebrations" be announced, and confessions heard, in the Establishment in 1890. Why, the Arians in their day had
Bishops, and Masses, and organization as perfect
as that of the orthodox ; but it was with Athanasius
that Newman ranged himself while still an Anglican ; and it was precisely the parallel he found
between Anglicans and Arians or Donatists that
brought him at last from Oxford to Birmingham.
It was he, in truth, who said to Anglicans such as
these—

Look into the matter more steadily ; it is very pleasant to
decorate your chapels, oratories, and studies now, but you
cannot be doing this for ever. It is pleasant to adopt a
habit or a vestment ; to use your Office-book or your beads ;
but it is like feeding on flowers unless you have that objective
vision in your faith, and that satisfaction in your reason, of
which devotional exercises and ecclesiastical appointments
are the suitable expression. They will not last in the long
run, unless commanded and rewarded on Divine authority ;
they cannot be made to rest on the influence of individuals.
It is well to have rich architecture, curious works of art, and
splendid vestments, when you have a present God ; but oh,
what a mockery if you have not ! If your externals surpass
what is within, you are so far as hollow as your Evangelical
opponents, who baptize, yet expect no grace. Thus your
Church becomes not a home, but a sepulchre ; like those
high cathedrals once Catholic, which you do not know what

to do with, which you shut up, and make monuments of, sacred to the memory of what has passed away.

"You are under a destiny," very solemnly said Newman also to the Anglican clergy, after he had become a Catholic ; and he was attributing to them what he had always believed in a very special manner of himself. Not the third Napoleon himself had franker conviction of the distinctness of his fate. During the tour in the South of Europe, in 1833—the tour which produced "Lead, kindly Light"—"I began," he tells us, "to think that I had a mission." When he paused in Rome and was asked by Monsignor Wiseman to pay a second visit, he replied with great gravity, "I have a work to do in England." In Sicily, after an illness, he sat down on his bed and began to sob violently. "My servant asked what ailed me. I could only answer him, 'I have a work to do in England.'" The record, with the obvious hint, is made by himself ; and he evidently believed it to be no mere coincidence that his return home, with its strange adventures of both delay and speed, timed with Keble's sermon on "National Apostasy." It was the first Sunday after his arrival ; and he says, "I have ever considered this day as the start of the religious movement of 1833." When he retired to Littlemore, as a sort of half-way house between

England and Rome, he turned up an old copy-book, and it took his breath away to find on it a cross drawn between the words "verse" and "book." Moreover, a further device, in which one less smitten with his destiny might have recognized a sister's chain and pendant, he could not make out to be anything but "a set of beads with a little cross." Then there came his reception into the Catholic Church, and thus the man of destiny records it: "I am this night expecting Father Dominic the Passionist, who from his youth has been led to have distinct and direct thoughts, first, of the countries of the north, and then of England. After thirty years' (almost) waiting, he was, without his own act, sent here." This is in the "Apologia;" and in "Loss and Gain," under fictitious names, the story is told in greater detail :—

On the Apennines, near Viterbo, there dwelt a shepherd boy, in the first years of this century, whose mind had early been drawn heavenward ; and one day, as he prayed before an image of the Madonna, he felt a vivid intimation that he was to preach the Gospel under the northern sky. There appeared no means by which a Roman peasant should be turned into a missionary ; nor did the prospect open, when this youth found himself, first, a lay brother, then a Father, in the Congregation of the Passion. Yet, though no external means appeared, the inward impression did not fade—on the contrary, it became more definite ; and, in process of time, instead of the dim north, England was engraven on his heart. And, strange to say, as years went on, without his seeking, for he was simply under obedience, our peasant found himself at length upon the very shore of the stormy Northern Sea, whence Cæsar of old looked out for a new world to conquer; yet that he should cross the Strait was still as little likely as before. But the day came, not, however, by any determination of his own, but by the same Providence which, thirty years before, had given him the intimation of it.

The importance which each Christian must of necessity attach to himself—he for whom the Heavens descended to the earth, who has angels for his ministers, who is an heir of Paradise, and who traces the special designs of Providence in the details of his daily life—might seem to be alien to the humility and to the self-abnegation which Christianity enjoins. Yet he, whose Christian egoism is most sublime, he it is who, paradoxically, abases and annihilates himself most completely. " From a boy I had been led to consider that my Maker and I, His creature, were the two beings, luminously such." And the attitude remained to the end, and determined the disposition of Newman towards all people and things. " It is face to face in all matters between man and his God. He alone creates ; He alone has redeemed ; before His awful eyes we go in death ; and in the vision of Him is our eternal beatitude."

But those who came near to the Sacred Person

had reflections of His glory, and as such were held in worship by Newman—the angels and the saints. And the men about himself he frankly regarded in the light of their relations, not with the outer world, but with him and his spiritual being. The record of his Oxford contemporaries is the record of what they were to him, "John Henry Newman." He learnt, for instance, habits of thought and the idea of the Church as a corporate body from Whately; Hurrell Froude "fixed deep in me the idea of devotion to the Blessed Virgin, and led me gradually to believe in the Real Presence;" Keble familiarized him with the sacramental system; and from Dr. Hawkins he learnt the value of tradition. The bond was a close one in all cases; but it had its basis on religion. In the streets of Dublin, long after, Whately as Archbishop, and Newman as Rector of the Catholic University, met without recognition; but the story of his having absented himself, years before, from chapel on purpose to avoid receiving the Sacrament with Dr. Whately, was pure invention. "He made himself dead to me," says Newman of Whately with great simplicity; adding, "My reason told me it was impossible we could have got on together longer had he stayed in Oxford; yet I loved him too much to bid him farewell without pain." When Kingsley

said, "Truth for its own sake had never been a
virtue with the Roman clergy," and this in a mere
magazine with the poor life of a month in it, no
one would have bothered his head over it—the
charge was too hackneyed to need a new rebuff
from Catholics. But "Father Newman" was
linked with the passage, fortunately, as he himself
afterwards thought. He accuses "me, John Henry
Newman," exclaimed the hermit at Birmingham,
whose destiny the Heavens had made known to
him.

So the "Apologia" was written. Later on, the
passages which seemed to have personal resentment were suppressed by the author; who, moreover, gave the Rev. Sir William Cope a most
interesting explanation of his adoption of the
world's own weapons—hard words—in the unequal
duel: the world would not believe him if he spoke
calmly. His after-thoughts were that Kingsley
should escape resentment because he had become
accidentally "the instrument in the good Providence
of God, by whom I had an opportunity given me,
which otherwise I should not have had, of vindicating my character and conduct in my 'Apologia.'"
Not, as he might well have said, "vindicating the
Catholic doctrine as to truth, and the sin of lying;"
but vindicating, what with Newman was a synonym,

" my character and conduct." And Newman adds, in the same letter, that a friend had chanced to hear Kingsley " preaching about me kindly ; " and about Athanasius, too, he had been writing less unkindly ; so " I said Mass for his soul as soon as I heard of his death."

The old friends he lost and the new friends he made when he became a Catholic were they whom " *God* gave me when *He* took every one else away." " And in you, Ambrose St. John," that chief new friend, he says, " I gather up and bear in memory those familiar and affectionate companions and counsellors who in Oxford *were given to me* to be my daily solace and relief ; and all those others, of great name and high example, who were my thorough friends ; and also those many younger men, whether I knew them or not, who have never been disloyal to me by word or deed." To Pius IX. he paid his homage in a sermon at Birmingham, in which he recalls "his great act towards us here, towards me." " One of his first acts after he was Pope was, in his great condescension, to call me to Rome ; then, when I got there, he bade me send for my friends to be with me ; and he formed us into an Oratory. . . . Such is the Pope now happily reigning in the Chair of St. Peter ; such are our personal obligations to

him ; such has he been towards us, towards you,
my brethren."

It was precisely this pervading personality in
Newman that distinguished him from his contemporaries. The pretentious "we" was dropped
in favour of the simpler "I." The abstract was
exchanged for the concrete under a pen primed
with individuality. The unit spoke to the unit—
to the units who made up mankind. "Heart
speaketh unto heart," was his own chosen motto as
a Cardinal, who bared his heart for the inspection
of friend and foe ; who told men how, when he
was ordained an Anglican minister, "he wept most
abundant and most sweet tears at the thought of
what he had then become," and so on, through all
the phases of his life. Only those entirely ignorant
of Newman's selflessness in conduct would put down
this self-analysis and self-centred measurement of
men to petty vanity, from which he was wholly
free, or to vulgar love of applause, of which he
had none. For the most part the poet alone has
shown himself so spontaneously, so autobiogra-
phically in his manuscripts ; and all the world has
listened. But here, at last, humanity could be
studied in a priest. The personal and the human
had re-inhabited poetry with Shelley, Keats, and
Wordsworth ; and with Newman the personal and

the human entered into theology, and into his account of it. He allowed himself to be put under the microscope, and how he bore the ordeal all his contemporaries will tell.

Yet Newman's friendships, though formed and governed under exacting and unusual conditions, were extraordinarily tender. Such friendships among men were less common when the Oxford movement began than they have since become ; and the present generation, if it owed nothing else to the *Newmania* (as Bishop Hampden called it), would have reason to be grateful for this infusion of tenderness into the relations of man with man. The sentiment expressed, to George Eliot's great admiration, in the closing passage of the "Apologia," appears and reappears elsewhere—in Newman's method of addressing Dr. Church, Dean of St. Paul's—"*Carissime ;*" in his sudden outbreak where, on hearing of the death of Hurrell Froude, he throws aside in one epithet the conventional stiffness of the eighteenth century which ruled nearly all his poems, and exclaims—

> "*Dearest!* he longs to speak, as I to know,
> And yet we both refrain ;
> It were not good : a little doubt below,
> And all will soon be plain."

Newman's young men improved on their model.

Faber, who had a greater exuberance of both
feeling and expression, wrote to the present Duke
of Rutland, then Lord John Manners—

> " Thou walkest with a glory round thy brow,
> Like saints in pictures, radiant in the blaze
> And splendour of thy boyhood, mingling now
> With the bold bearing of a man, that plays
> In eyes, which do with such sweet skill express
> Thy soul's hereditary gentleness."

That male eyes had " sweet skill," or that men
had eyes at all worth observing by men, came as
a surprise, if not as a shock, to many ; and Faber
himself, writing to some one who expostulated
with him, says : " Strong expressions towards male
friends are matters of taste. I feel what they
express to me. B. thinks a revival of chivalry
in male friendships a characteristic of the rising
generation, and a hopeful one." " B.," whoever he
was, was right. The shyness which made an
Englishman ashamed to embrace even his father,
arose from times when wine-parties and a common
interest in the heredity of dogs and horses were
the most sacred links between men. The Oxford
movement established different relations—of mutual
confidence, mutual affection, mutual respect. Of
the influence for good which these generous friendships exercised, Mark Pattison was sensible—and
even Mr. James Anthony Froude. At first, when

undergraduates went home raving about Newman, anxious parents shook their heads. The correspondence passing about the same date between Lord Strangford and the old Duke of Rutland, reveals the perturbations of aristocratic fathers over the friendships between their sons and the plain commoner who was afterwards to make his Queen an Empress, his solicitor a baronet, and his secretary a peer. So of Newman, the fountain of so much piety for thirsty souls in future, anxious mothers were asking, "But is he a *good* man ?" And, "But is he a good man ?" diffident fathers and confiding sisters chimed in. When the sermons and tracts penetrated into the provinces, the question answered itself; and happy were the mothers whose sons were under the influence which made religion seem to the young, and even to the ambitious, something manly and ennobling.

It was near Windermere that Charlotte Brontë, as the guest of the Shuttleworths in 1850, met her future biographer, and told her during their first talk "about Father Newman's lectures at the Oratory in a very concise, graphic way." Then follow some dots, eloquent dots. What do they conceal? Probably some phrase not much more reasonable than Carlyle's description of Newman

as possessing "the brain of a medium-sized rabbit."
For Charlotte Brontë combined, as no mind, thanks
largely to Newman, ever will again in England,
exquisite sensibility, deep religiousness, and an
open intelligence, with as strained a notion of
Popery as that of any Exeter Hall rhetorician.
"Good people—very good people—I doubt not,
there are among the Romanists," she says in a
weakly generous mood ; " but," she makes haste to
add, writing to Mrs. Gaskell, who discovered lean-
ings to primitive Christianity, "but the system is
not one which should have such sympathy as
*yours.* Look at Popery taking off the mask at
Naples." The last sentence reads like the text
of one of Newman's lectures, a text to be torn
mercilessly to tatters.

By the way, Miss Brontë and Mrs. Gaskell went
to tea at this time at Fox How, the house of the
widow of Dr. Arnold ; and Mrs. Arnold had
yielded her son Thomas to follow Newman to
Rome. They were all in a tale, especially in
homes of hereditary goodness. When, at the very
beginning of things, Newman visited old Mr.
Wilberforce, and saw his pious family, little did
this pattern of Evangelicalism suppose that out
of four sons three would become Catholics, leaving
only Samuel to adorn the Anglican bench, while

his unworldly brothers went their simple ways—
one, Archdeacon Robert Isaac Wilberforce, to die
while preparing for the priesthood in Rome;
another, William, "the squire," to spend an obscure
life as a Catholic layman; and the third, Henry—
most delightful of them all—to found the *Weekly
Register*, in this as in all else, says Newman,
" actuated by an earnest desire to promote the
interests of religion, though at the sacrifice of his
own." What is recorded of the Scotts, the
Arnolds, and the Wilberforces, is recorded of nearly
every family in England. Lord Coleridge, who
never showed a nobler figure than when he knelt
by the coffin of the Cardinal in the dreary church
at Birmingham, must have thought of his own
brother—a Jesuit priest; and Lord / Selborne,
lamenting Newman as the father of modern
Anglicanism, counted a brother among the band
of Newman's closer followers to Rome.

Nor was this influence confined to those who
came within the magic of Newman's personality,
or to those who were students rather than hard-
headed men of the world; or yet to men of his
own generation. When a typical Yorkshireman,
like Lord Ripon, with all the best qualities and
sympathies which distinguish John Bull, appeared
at the London Oratory to claim admission to the

Catholic Church, it was to the writings of Newman
that he attributed the transition which so greatly
perturbed the mind of Mr. Gladstone. Yet even
Mr. Gladstone, when he wrote bitterly of all others,
said of Newman that, honoured as he was, he
illustrated the line that "the world knows nothing
of its greatest men." Newman returned the compliment by speaking of Mr. Gladstone's as "so
religious a mind." But Newman also accused
Anglicans, in one of his lectures to them, of
"praising this or that Catholic saint, to make up
for abuse, and to show your impartiality." Whether
Mr. Gladstone will plead guilty to this indictment
I cannot say ; but if he will look at his various and
most welcome praises of Newman, and see how, by
juxtaposition, they are made to imply dispraise of
the brother and colleague bearing the burden of
government and the responsibility of the bishopric,
he will not wonder at the words of Newman coming
to his reader's mind.

Indeed, the throwing together of the names of
the two Cardinals has been a common feat of
jugglery vainly performed to annihilate the one or
the other. It is delightful, despite all differences
of temperament, and of the objectivity and the
subjectivity with which each variously regarded
the outer world, to see these two names linked

together, if not in daily speech, in the unity of eternal love. When Newman was twenty-eight, the younger man of twenty was led captive by the "form and voice and penetrating words at Evensong in the University Church at Oxford;" where, having once seen and heard Newman, he "never willingly failed to be." When the fury of officialdom in the Anglican Church was fulminating against Littlemore, Manning, the born administrator, the bright hope of officialdom, wherever he was found, paid a conspicuous visit of sympathy to its occupant—though his thoughts just then were not the thoughts of Newman, especially as to Rome. This was what the Cardinal Archbishop was thinking of when he said at the Requiem at the London Oratory: "And when trials came I was not absent from him. Littlemore is before me now as fresh as yesterday." The next time they met was in Rome, when Newman was first dressed as an Oratorian, and then, five years later, the future Archbishop, having himself become a Catholic, listened once more to the "well-known voice, sweet as of old, but strong in the absolute truth, prophesying a second spring, in the first Provincial Council of Westminster." In 1857, Newman dedicated to Cardinal Manning his volume of "Sermons on Various Occasions," "as some memorial of the friendship there has been between us for nearly thirty years ;" and in 1861 the compliment was returned, Cardinal Manning testifying : " To you I owe a debt of gratitude, for intellectual light and help, greater than to any one man of our time." There the matter may be left, under the hands that have never signed insincerities. What if, between two men of character so marked, there were light difficulties in the way of a continual and close interchange of thoughts and emotions? Only the vulgar can demand of men a contact contrary to temperament, or will profess to be astonished, if Cardinal Newman's most intimate and frequent letters are not found to be indited to his brother Cardinal ; nor even to Father Faber, that " bright, particular star," revolving round Newman by a force greater than he could control.

Lord Beaconsfield, when he said, a generation later than 1845, that the Anglican Church still reeled under the secession of Dr. Newman, was looking at it politically ; and he pronounced it, with all the assurance of Downing Street, to be " a blunder." Lord John Russell probably combined private with public feeling when he alluded in Parliament, in 1851, to " a person of great eminence, of great learning, of great talents, whom we all

I

have to deplore as having left the Protestant
Church, and joined the Church of Rome—I mean,
Mr. Newman." The busy world went on. It
wondered a moment at the great renunciation; and
then it lost sight of the neophyte. But it heard
of him again; and the day came when he had
leavened the whole Establishment, and when his
voice held men of many minds and all communions
as by a spell. From Lord Coleridge and Mr. John
Morley, from Dean Church and Mr. Kegan Paul,
from Mr. R. H. Hutton and Mr. Froude, from Mr.
Frederic Harrison and Mr. Matthew Arnold (who
says that beside Newman's style Ruskin's is provincial), from Mr. Augustine Birrell and Mr. W.
E. Henley, from Mr. Aubrey de Vere and Mr.
Burnand, from Miss Christina Rossetti and Dean
Stanley, from Sir Francis Doyle and Lord Blach-
ford, from Professor St. George Mivart and Principal
Shairp, from all the critics of all the schools
and all the creeds, came one concordant voice in
praise of John Henry Newman as author and as
man.

> " Sweetly the light
> Shines from the solitary peak at Edgbaston,"

sang Coventry Patmore, who understood that even
the polemical pamphleteer of 1874 had "peace in
heart" though "wrath in hand," and that his most

trenchant paragraphs were the "gold blazonries of Love irate," and never "the black flag of Hate."

These names represent "light and leading," men with minds and pens "beautiful and swift." But, O phenomenon! the mass walked and even ran with its masters. The young lions of the *Daily Telegraph* roared out praise. James Macdonell, the type in sayings and doings of everything Newman was not, avows that his "admiration for the saint-like beauty of Newman's character, for the exquisite character of his genius, for his wonderful insight into human nature, for his marvellous command over the resources of the literary art, is such that I never think of him without mentally lifting my hat in token of my reverence." He was "specially fond of reading Newman's writings aloud on Sunday afternoons," and "his favourite hymn was 'Lead, kindly Light!'" Yet, "it is the testimony of her who knew him best that the question of his own salvation never troubled him." So it happens that many admired Newman for his accidents and his accessories, without even hearing the essential message of his life. That can be best summed up in the words he once addressed to the Anglican clergy: "I want to make you anxious about your souls." And vain as in death would all praise have sounded on his ears that was not based on the recognition of this as his only hope and ambition; of this as the end for which he wrote as fervently, as individually, as he prayed.

THE END.

PRINTED BY WILLIAM CLOWES AND SONS, LIMITED,
LONDON AND BECCLES.